The Story of the Children of Joseph Jarrell Sinclair and Lula Kate Evans, Welch, Sinclair

Don Sinclair

Copyright © 2021 by Don Sinclair

All rights reserved. No part of this publication may be reproduced, distributed, or transmitted in any form or by any means, including photocopying, recording, or other electronic or mechanical methods, without the prior written permission of the publisher, except in the case brief quotations embodied in critical reviews and other noncommercial uses permitted by copyright law.

ISBN: 978-1-63945-148-7 (Paperback)
    978-1-63945-149-4 (Ebook)

The views expressed in this book are solely those of the author and do not necessarily reflect the views of the publisher, and the publisher hereby disclaims any responsibility for them.

Writers' Branding
1800-608-6550
www.writersbranding.com
orders@writersbranding.com

The Story of the Children of

Joseph Jarrell Sinclair and Lula Kate Evans, Welch, Sinclair

By Donald Wood Sinclair

Photo of Lula Kate Sinclair and Joseph Jarrell Sinclair

I was the surprise birth to middle-age parents Joseph Jarrell Sinclair and Lula Kate Evens, Welch, Sinclair. I was their fourth child together. My father did not think he would live long enough to see me grown. He was 45 years old when I was born, October 6, 1929 in Minden, Texas. I was 45 years old when he died near the age of 90 years.

This document is the story about my relationship to my father and mother and our family of 10 children growing up in east Texas. There was another child born to my father and his first wife in 1910 that lived only one year. I had never heard about her until I went home to get all the names straight. My mother remembered this child born to my father and his first wife. Her name was Mary Sinclair.

Joseph Sinclair was 9 years older than Lula Kate Welch. He was a cotton farmer in Minden, Texas, Rusk County. His farm was about 2 miles west of Minden. He was a respected community leader and a successful farmer. He first married a young woman from the Barton family in Minden. Lula Kate was the daughter of the owner of the huge 2-story store located in the middle of Minden. She kept the books for her father and helped him keep up with restocking his huge store. She was also a school teacher. She first married a tall young man named Bentley Welch.

Joseph had 5 children and Lula Kate had 1 child before the flu epidemic at the end of World War I (about 1918) took both their partner's lives. Joe was on the School Board that hired Lula Kate to teach, and it didn't take him long to realize he needed Lula Kate to help him raise his and her children. So, they married and Lula Kate gave up her teaching career to make a home for all six of their children plus the 4 she bore to Joe in the next few years. I was the last one of those four.

Lula Kate turned to housekeeping, cooking, and washing all those children's clothes and being a mother to them all. Joe's oldest daughter, Syble, was only 9 years younger than Lula Kate, but mom told me Syble was always very helpful to her in the many tasks and responsibilities with the children and the house. I was glad she told me that, because I didn't like Syble as I grew up. I'll share more on that later in this paper.

So, I was Lula Kate's baby boy. That means I had her at home when all the others were off in school. I will be sharing with you some of my strong ideas that developed early in my life. I will begin by sharing some of the relationships within my family that I consider significant.

My oldest half-brother, Marion Sebastian Sinclair, was probably the sorriest human being I have ever met. During the worst depression ever known (1930) he made $300 per month as head driller on oil rigs. Between jobs he would disappear with the money and show up a few days later unable to pay his grocery bill. He would flop on the bed and go to sleep. Once I saw his wife, Louise Lawrence, take a razor strap in both hands and lay it into his back. It popped like a gun shot. He got up, chased her down and beat on her for a while before returning to sleep. My father always blamed Louise as the problem, but I knew she was never treated right by her husband usually called "Boots". Their 4 children were my playmates and friends. I was always very fond of all of them.

My father would have to pay their grocery bill so Louise could get food for his grandchildren. On many occasions, my mother would place a large flat pan filled with biscuits and gravy on my lap and my father would drive me 4 miles to provide them food before going to school. Their home was my father's old home in which I was born. They lived there rent free. Their oldest child was Virginia, the sweetest woman I have ever known. In self-defense Louise divorced my half-brother and took the children to Houston. She found defense work during WWII and finally remarried to a nice man. I always loved Louise and her children. Virginia spent several months in our home to finish school. They were all very special to me.

Boots, that half-brother with more money than the rest of us, refused to pay child support on their children. If he came back into Texas to work on a well and Louise heard about it, she would call the authorities and have him put in jail. He would call our father and ask him for the money to get out of jail telling my father he had paid the child support and had the receipts. My father would believe him and criticize Louise for causing all the trouble. Lula, my mother, but not Boots', would try to tell my father that if he had the receipts, he would not be in jail. To which my father would get louder in his criticism of Louise as the 'trouble maker' and bail Boots out again. I suppose everyone is entitled to one major imperfection, but I just never could grant my father the right to that one. That happened many times exactly the same way. I do not buy this adage that the first 'boy' always gets the best deal in the family. This borders closer to the line I think of as insanity.

Boots injured his left arm seriously on the job and was not able to work for the big money any longer. He met a very ugly woman in Houston out drinking with his brother Joe Everitt. Boots and Athine were both alcoholics but they decided to stop drinking and support each other. He brought her back to Henderson and talked one of my classmates into letting him remodel an old run-down tourist court my classmate had bought to open another used car lot on later. Boots and girlfriend, Athine, lived there for several years and were very happy. Boots' children actually grew fond of Athine because the two were so happy for so long together, and they had helped each other stop drinking.

One Sunday morning, Boots, who had worked around dangerous machinery all his life, went out to adjust the trip switch that lowered the bed on a dump truck he had bought to make extra money. He attempted to adjust the switch without propping the bed up. The bed dropped on him killing him instantly. Athine took it real hard, and Boots' kids tried to maintain relationship with her. But Boots' son stopped by on his way home early one evening and found her drunk and in bed with a traveling bug exterminator who had rented a cabin from her. Athine was so embarrassed and hurt, and Boots' children were so disturbed by it that it tore apart the good relationship they all had.

Syble and Frankie were my two half-sisters from Joseph's group. They were both married before I was old enough to know them. We went to visit Syble when I was about eight years old. We went to the beach at Goose Creek, Texas. Today it is called Baytown.

A lady on the beach was floating on two inner tubes that fit inside a nylon cover. She asked me if I would play with her float while she went up the beach to get a hot dog. I have never enjoyed doing anyone a favor as much as I enjoyed getting my hands on that marvelous float. When she got back, I immediately brought her float back to her, but she asked me to keep it while she ate her hot dog.

Syble saw me pick up the float at that point and start back toward the water with it. She came running down to the beach and began to spank me shouting, "Sinclairs do not beg things off people!" The lady tried to explain, but Syble just kept spanking me. She hurt me! I had on a tight-fitting small bathing suit, and her angry spanking kept me from explaining I did not beg that float off the lady. Syble was so angry and wild that we had to take down our tent, load everything in the car and go home. Sinclairs really do not beg things off people, but I am glad all Sinclairs do not jump to conclusions like Syble did when people involved were trying so hard to offer her a different understanding of what happened.

I have never explained that horrible experience to Syble, but I didn't like her even a little bit. An opportunity to really slam into her came at the Sinclair's home dinner table in 1951. I was grown, married, and the Pastor of a small Methodist Church. The end of my mother's dining table was pushed against the wall. My wife and I sat against the wall on one side and Syble and her husband sat on the other side against the wall. Syble began condemning all the different churches and calling them the hardest people to get along with or live with in the world.

I began to look around that dining table. Her husband beside her, one of the finest men I have ever known, would never go with her to these churches she got involved with. My half-brother Vance was next and he had never joined any church. Next around the dining table was our father who sometimes went to special events at mom's church, but had never joined a church.

So, when Syble took a breath, I said, "Syble, I believe that I could go around this table and get everyone here to agree that the hardest people to get along with in this world is irrational and judgmental people like you!"

Syble jumped to her feet and started around that table to get at me. But her husband surprised us all by catching her arm and pulling her back to her chair and forcing her to sit down saying, "Where are you going, Honey?" Syble said, "Do you think I'm going to sit here and take that off that stupid little brother?" Her husband said, "Honey what he said to you is 30 years past due.!" Syble began to cry. My wife, Kathy, whose family was peaceful about everything, claims that event caused her to give birth to our first child, David, that night at 4:10 AM.

I have been glad this event ended like it did because I was grown now and would have enjoyed hurting Syble if she had made it around that table. I have never hit a woman, but I would have enjoyed hitting and hurting Syble that day. I never did tell her why I despised her so much. I hate injustice and am always ready to correct it when I can. Syble was married to a big strong man we all liked and appreciated the fact that he never got involved in her silly religious relationships. I lost a 5-cents bet to him during the middle 1930s when Joe Louis was in the boxing ring with the German heavyweight champion Max Schmelling. The German was outboxing Joe Louis, a black American Champion. I was about eight years old and made a remark about it wouldn't be long before Joe Louis would get knocked out. Bear, Syble's husband's nickname, disagreed. He said Joe Louis had such a strong right-hand punch that he would hit the German with before long that would knock the German out. We agreed on a 5-cent bet on our opinions. It wasn't long before Joe Louis landed that powerful right-hand punch. Down went the German.

Bear was famous in our county as a young man for being able to get a full bail of cotton on his back and carry it 50 yards. He was a very good quiet husband to Syble. I always had great respect for him. They had two daughters. Nancy married locally, but the 2nd daughter went to Louisiana State University. When Syble learned she was dating a foreigner from Central America who was Roman Catholic, she rushed into LSU, snatched the 2nd daughter up, and took her home.

They came to visit us at Minden, Texas together. I didn't know this daughter well at all, and she just sat quietly around without talking to anyone. I knew her mother had jumped on her very hard. I had her mother do that to me very unjustly. But I did not get a chance to talk with her at our home. When she promised her mother, she would break it off with the Roman Catholic young man from Central America her mother took her back to LSU. At which time this 2nd daughter married this terrible Roman Catholic young man and immediately moved to Central America—completely out of reach of her mother. We came to know the young man was from the "moneyed" families in Central America with ownership of plantations and businesses. So, her family was wealthy in a land that had a lot of poverty that never seemed to improve through the years.

About 15 or more years ago I learned that her family had to leave Central America because the poor people were revolting and it was dangerous for her family to live there. Her family had moved north to an island nation to live for safety. She is the only member of my family that I have ever heard of moving because they had all the money and people around them were starving.

Syble's older daughter is Nancy. She actually married a man named Turnipseed. He is a fine man, and Nancy has had a long marriage that's getting longer by the years. She also had a good supply of common sense that I have enjoyed in the very few conversations I have had with her. Once, a few years ago now, I stopped by to see her. In a conversation, I said, "Your mother (Syble) was not fair about that situation." To which she turned from something she was doing as we talked and said, "Don, my mother was never fair about anything!"

She also told about sitting on our back steps (about 12 steps high) as a young girl waiting to watch me jump the 3 barbed wired fences as I ran home from school at lunchtime. She thought that was so wonderful for me to be able to jump those fences that she waited eagerly to greet me as I ran up the high step system she was sitting on. She said, "You always just kept going up the stairs past me without saying a word." She was always so disappointed.

My response to her was equally revealing. "Nancy, I was 15/16 years old, and I was afraid of girls then." But she felt it was a personal "put down" to her for me to ignore her that way. I apologized to her because I really thought she was always such a nice person. I have wondered sometimes about how much she had to handle growing up in Syble's and Bear's families. Maybe Bear was more helpful to a young girl. Anyway, Nancy turned out to be able to handle it objectively and make a wonderful life for herself in spite of whatever she had to deal with as Syble's daughter.

Frankie was the pretty half-sister in the family. She was not as helpful to my mother as Syble was. She avoided washing dishes or doing anything that might scratch her nails. She complained that our dad didn't have a nicer car for the family. His work was handling the Oldsmobile Dealer's used car lot for a few years before he retired. He really came home with some surprises. He would keep fairly useful vehicles for our use even though they did not look so good. I often drove a 1932 Ford pickup he rigged with a wire pull starter after you twisted the two naked wires together inside. It was very rusty, but I got the job of hauling firewood to the school to keep the students warm after our biggest building burned. I was paid $8 a load. My father was chairman of the School Board when the need arose. I also learned how to get a loaded log truck or a pickup loaded with firewood unstuck that got stuck far from a road. I had to learn how to believe in possibilities that others could not readily see. That has served me well in many ways all my life. When everyone else is giving up I do not. I have accomplished many things that others see as impossible.

But Frankie didn't even want to ride in these wonderful vehicles. My father could have bought better cars, but he just let his children drive them or make what they wanted to out of them.

Frankie married a really good-looking man who was the butcher in a grocery store. After several years of marriage, her Bill got the woman at the cash register pregnant. They divorced and Bill married the other woman. The child was a girl. I think the mother soon died of an illness. Frankie moved back home after her divorce and continued in college and finished her degree to teach. She and I would sit at the same table and do our homework by lamplight. We were real friends.

Once I dropped by her home where she lived alone, and there sat Bill. I had always liked him. He seemed like a nice man, but he had messed up several people's lives. My visits with Frankie were to quiz her about her plans and I asked the question about her having to go to school this summer or not. She said, "Bill and I are talking about trying again. Are you going to run me off?"

I was the only Pastor in the family and none of my family knew how to relate to me. They would call my mother to ask what kind of behavior they should exhibit around me. My response to my friend Frankie was, "No! I'm not going to run you off. I think that is a good idea. You have not even dated other men at all, and Bill came straight to you when he could."

So, a few months later, a friend drove them and several members of Bill's family to Palestine, Texas and I presided over the second marriage of Frankie Sinclair and Bill Armstrong in my living room. And another beautiful thing began to take place. Frankie and Bill's 20-year-old daughter developed a very special and close friendship that continued long after Bill died. I do not know where she is now. I do not remember her name. I do know that she is living as a well-beloved daughter of Bill and Frankie Armstrong. And, I do know that I am really happy about that.

Vance Sinclair, the quiet member of my father's older children, was a really good man. I have seen him show tremendous respect and consideration for other people many times. He earned good salaries working on oil rigs regularly. His failings show up when he was not working. He would allow a bunch of guys going to find illegal or legal whiskey and get drunk to talk him into going along. He always had money enough to pay his part, so, his buddies liked to have him come along.

He joined the United States Cavalry when I was a kid. We drove into Louisiana once to see him when his Unit was down there practicing being the Cavalry. Their horses seemed really big to me. When World War II began, he immediately reenlisted and was sent to New Zealand to fight in the Pacific with the First Marine Division as General MacArthur was preparing to push the Japanese off the islands all the way to past The Philippine Islands. Vance made three of the landings with these Marine Divisions without being injured, but he came home with Malaria. He joked about being in the "dismounted" Cavalry.

Frankie was home following her unhappy divorce situation. She and I were sitting at a card table with a kerosene lamp before us doing homework. Vance was sitting on a sofa next to us. He had just 'slept off' his latest night out with the boys drinking. He suddenly crushed the newspaper he was reading down onto his lap and said, "Sis, I've got $800 in the bank that I'm going to get for you tomorrow. You will make good use of it, and if I keep it, I'll just drink it up!" He got the money and gave it to her to help with the educational costs to finish her degree.

When I arrived home from overseas with the Air Force, he immediately gave me the keys to his car, saying, "You might need a car for a while more than I do. I can catch a ride to work." I was driving his car in Henderson, Texas (Uptown for folks in Minden). I decided to circle the 'square' looking things over, and I spotted him leaning against a light pole on the corner of a deserted city square. When he got into the car, he said, "Little brother, I'm going to ask you to take me somewhere to get something, and then ask you to forget you ever took me there." He wanted to pick up a couple of his buddies and some 'moonshine' whiskey. But he did not want me to ever be involved in anything like that. He respected what I was planning for my life.

Vance never wanted to have responsibility for another person's life, nor did he want a job 'over' other people. He was almost 'court-martialed' in the war because he would not accept the single stripe promotion to 'Private First Class'. He did not want to be responsible for sending other men into battle and get some of them killed.

Boots made a lot more salary than Vance ever did, but Vance was the family member 'Boots' would go to ask for money when he was broke. I wondered if Vance ever got paid back. I was standing talking to Vance one day when Boots came in, walked over to Vance, and asked to borrow $20.00 until payday. Vance just reached into his pocket, pulled out $20.00, and handed it to Boots. As Boots walked out, Vance said to me, "Little brother, there goes $20.00 I will never see again." He finished brushing his hair, placed the hairbrush on the dresser, patted me on the back, and went on with his day.

The "baby boy" in diapers my father had when Lula married Joseph was Joe Everitt. I have often wondered about the difference between Lula's children and all those from the Barton side—their mother. As a child, I knew the Bartons as not-to-be desired—at leased by me. At one event one of the younger Bartons hid in a weed patch with a shotgun in order to shoot some family member—I think it was his uncle—in the back. I am not sure what the issue was but it happened about 1938 or 1939. As a Sinclair, who would not even "beg" afloat off a beach lady, or ask for a drink of water away from home, such action was "outside" my thinking entirely. I didn't know many of the Barton's personally, but ALL of her children in my family were not normal, "good neighbor" citizens of the land. They were all difficult to relate to or get along with.

Joe Everitt was such a capable man, but his attitude toward everybody was so pathetic it was always surprising me. He sold "Hotshot" parts to "supe up" car motors. He traveled over half of Texas's 254 counties between El Paso, Dallas & Houston. He married a part-Indian woman from Oklahoma twice and divorced her twice. With her, he had one daughter who now lives in Houston. We are pretty good friends, but she wants to "help" me buy nicer shoes. And, she didn't even invite me to her last wedding a year or so ago. It could be because she married "outside" or "inside" some religion, or it could be she assumed I would be offended because she didn't ask me to officiate at her wedding. Who knows, but I am pleased that she keeps her business as "her business". I love the girl, but that is an "uphill" task sometimes. I just keep being reminded she is a "Barton" from Minden, Texas through her father. Back to Joe Everitt.

Joe Everitt worked hard to develop his business across Texas. He won awards in his company: was 'salesman of the year' more than once. The first time he was proud and brought the booklet around to show his family members. But, his friends kept asking, "Joe, why did you take your picture with your hat on?" He always hated that he was very bald by the age of 21. So, he stopped showing his picture so much and kept working hard on his business.

He went to a company New Year's Eve Party one year. This is the kind of party where the company furnishes the women. Joe got acquainted with Margaret—one of the women brought in. He took her home with him that night and kept her with him for about 6 or 8 years as his "traveling secretary". Margaret fitted right in. She worked as hard as he was working on his traveling business. She was really helpful to him, and he liked having her. When they came to Minden, Texas they never planned to spend the night. They were not married, and unmarried lovers were not supposed to sleep together at the Minden home of the parents.

Actually, my aging parents liked Margaret and would not have cared if Joe and Margaret used the same bedroom. But Joe felt he was breaking some rule he did not want to break. Then he up and bought Margaret a wedding ring and they had a wedding. It surprised us all. They bought a nice home in Houston I would visit sometimes. Joe Everitt liked me probably more than any of the other family members. We would talk together in his living room—Margaret was always in the kitchen. She didn't want anyone else in her kitchen.

One evening Joe's daughter had been around asking for some money. He said that was the only time he ever saw her—when she wanted some money. He wanted me to get out of my church work and work with him—guaranteed me a million dollars. I asked him why he felt he needed a million dollars, to which he replied, "So I can tell my neighbor to go straight to hell!" He did build an 8 ft high solid board fence out back so he could throw a rubber ball against it and his little house dogs could chase it. He insisted I was wasting my life, and nobody was going to appreciate it or care about it after it was wasted.

That night as he spoke of his daughter and continued his drinking, he began to cry between drinks. I realized that every day of my life would be a greater experience than any one of the days of his life.

At one point he decided he needed to go to the bathroom. All of a sudden here comes Margaret racing to kneel down behind my chair to say, "Don, I want to thank you for the way you talk back to Joe. No one else anywhere ever speaks back to his expressions about other people or sick ideas except you. I don't want Joe to ever know I said this to you, but I wanted to use this trip to the bathroom to thank you for doing what you do for him." Back to the kitchen she went as fast as she had come lest he would catch her talking privately to me. After Joe died a few years later, Margaret often consulted with me about how she should handle Joe's money or what she should do about my brother only 2 years older than I was. I'll tell his story later.

Now I must tell the story of my mother's son with Bentley Welch. Joe Welch was also in diapers when Lula Kate married Joseph Jarrell Sinclair. I stood at my mother's knee as the Baptist Pastor at Minden, Texas married Joe Welch to Lennis. Lennis was the perfect woman for any man 6 feet tall. She was a country girl who stood tall and straight. She had perfect manners and all the graces of a young woman. She wasn't just "pretty," she was a totally beautiful woman. I have never figured out why she was marrying my half-brother, Joe Welch.

Joe Welch was also tall and very proper. He was neat and dressed well. He graduated from Baylor University in Waco, Texas, went straight to Ma Bell in Dallas, and got a job that was the only job he ever had—it was a good job for 35 years. He served AT&T well and AT&T served him well. He helped the professional football people put their games on our TV sets.

He was a kind man and a good church member. All elderly ladies on his home street learned he could make their quirky TV straighten up and run better. Joe gladly responded to all their calls.

Lennis, my favorite family member, wanted children. But none were coming. So, she initiated the adoption of a young boy named Paul. Paul now lives north of Denton, Texas with Peggy, his wife of many years. They are doing well. I try to call every year or so. Paul is always surprised but glad. He and I became close friends while he was growing up. I stayed in Lennis and Joe's home every February when Perkins School of Theology brought to SMU three lecturers for a week's lectures. It was called Minister's Week, and many clergymen and others attended. Paul and I would find some time to spend together during these visits.

Joe and Lennis always came to Minden at Christmas time with the very best Christmas presents on the market. They brought bicycles, red wagons, radios, really wonderful presents to us younger Sinclair children. They both always worked and saved their money through many years. Lennis worked for years with Perking School of Theology handling problems the students ran into. Then she worked for 8- or 10-years directing SMU's fundraising and support from the business community of Dallas. She never just had a job—she was recruited to do high-level and serious things. She was good at all these things and did them for years. Joe always did well in his 1-lifetime job at AT&T. They both made good salaries and handled their incomes well.

So, what was missing? Joe Welch just had no personal power. How could a person be so successful and straight and narrow—high marks in any subject area but without any personal power. It was worse than a self-image problem. It had to do with his BEING. He just wasn't present in any situation as a BEING able to grasp the importance and participate in important situations. He wasn't "present" to himself as an important BEING. He could not see himself in his vast worth in the world just as a person. If he hadn't married this "Perfect" woman BEING, Lennis, I don't know what would have become of him. He could make a "shallow" conversation shallower. He could chat and laugh for 30 minutes about how long the penis was on Wilt Chamberlain, the super-tall basketball player. He could name the people who have seen it and it's like he wanted their autographs on a picture of it.

Lennis knew this about him. So did Paul, the son. I saw this teenage son, at the dinner table with me and his parents, slam the back of his hand across Joe's face with a demand that his father "just shut up!" It startled me and Lennis. Joe just gathered his ability to talk after such a blow, flubbered a few times then gathered himself to say things like, "Boy, you better quit that!" "You better not do that again!" "You hear me?" "You better not do that again!" That's all Joe could manage to say after his teenage son had just slammed the back of his hand hard across his face. What Joe was saying had no substance. Neither did his response to the situation have any substance. THERE WAS NO "BEING" IN THE MAN TO RESPOND!

Two other stories to show my relationship with Lennis and with Paul. When Lennis was making up Paul's bed she pulled some drugs out as she tucked the sheets. Her heart just sank. No one could have told her that her son was on drugs. That happened to "other" people—not her wonderful son. She did not tell Joe about it. She picked up the telephone and called me to ask what to do in such a situation.

I helped her realize that he might still be that sweet, smart, young son of which she was so proud. So, have faith in him. Do not accuse him of anything. Simply ask him to sit down with you and talk to you about what had happened, and ask him if he would explain the drugs to you.

She used the rest of his day at school to practice calmly as a caring mother trusting her son to just tell her about the drugs. It worked really well. He had heard that you could buy drugs all over the place at school, and he just decided to try buying some to see if that were true. It worked, but he didn't know what to do with the drugs after he owned some. He said he certainly wasn't going to take the drugs, so he just slipped them under his mattress and forgot about them. He asked her to help him get rid of them. They decided together to flush them into the commode, which they did. They also embraced over the commode and each thanked the other for trusting and believing in the other. She thanked him for being such a trustworthy son and he thanked her for being such a trusting mother. Lennis called me just crying tears of joy thanking me for helping her be the mother Paul needed her to be.

On another of my visits to Dallas, Paul had expressed concern that he could not make the basketball team in Junior High School. The problem was he could not make the ball go in the goal from under the basket. He and I went out to his basketball goal to talk practically about shooting from under the goal. Paul was tall and they could get him the ball, but he just could not get the ball to go into the goal. So, we centered on how the goal was constructed to receive the ball if the shooter got the ball off the backboard just right. We drew an imaginary square above the goal where it is bolted to the backboard. Then we experimented with what angle would make a goal from what direction and what angle would not work and why. If the shooter was forced to shoot from in front of the goal where the ball had to hit the backboard in order to score. If the shooter was forced to shoot from either side, the ball would go in the goal if the ball were bounced off the backboard in only certain places.

Paul practiced using our experiment and immediately made the Jr. High basketball team. So, I must be a genius. If you do not believe this, just talk to Paul Welch.

After a very useful life with Lennis, Joe developed Parkinson's disease and finally became unmanageable for Lennis at home. Joe moved 6 miles away to a Methodist facility with Parkinson's disease to spend 20 years before he died there. Lennis went there to supervise his care almost every day for those 20 years. Paul's work was 100 miles north of Dallas, but he came to Dallas every Sunday to take his mother to their church, cut her grass, and trim all her plants in her yard. He treated her like the sweet mother she had been to him. He is the kind of son every parent wants. I wish him the very best for the rest of his life and hope Peggy realizes what a fine man and basketball player she has married. I think she is very aware of it and appreciates it.

This was the pattern of Lennis's and Paul's lives for many years until Lennis died in her mid-nineties.

Now for the younger set of children born to Lula Kate Sinclair and Joseph Jarrell Sinclair. Lucy Elizabeth Sinclair was my mother's only girl. She was born in 1921 and died in 1934 of pneumonia. She was talked about as being beautiful and a very sweet person loved by all who knew her. She took care of me sometimes. I remember grabbing at her as she leaped over the bed she was trying to make up. I grabbed for her and caught hold of her 'half' petticoat. My grab pulled her petticoat down low, and she got very angry with me for doing that.

Another time, in the huge kitchen my grandfather had built, mom was making an Indian costume for my 1st-grade brother. Lucy and I were just watching. The material my mother was using was a burlap feed sack that was a very coarse material that did not sew well at all. When mom pulled it over my brother's head to try it on him, Lucy laughed out. My brother got furious at her for laughing at him, but you know how that kind of thing is. You just can't hold it back. Lucy had to pick me up and take me out of the room because she couldn't stop laughing at my brother in that partly finished Indian costume.

Then abruptly, Lucy died from pneumonia when she was 14 years old. The loss of this beautiful and perfect daughter almost killed my mother. She cried in bed for a month. Neighbors came in to take care of me. I remember one of them picking me up and holding me high enough so I could see my mother lying in bed just crying her eyes out over her loss. I can still see that view 88 years later. I was glad when Tobe Wells Sinclair, my mother's next child after Lucy, named his first daughter Lucy.

Tobe was everybody's favorite person, too. He was a gentleman and a scholar. He was kind and helpful to other people. He protected me. Once, on the playground after school, Tobe was practicing his pitching the softball. I was there watching some of the other guys practicing when two older boys a short distance away got into a fight. One of them picked up a bat and hit the other one in the head knocking him down. Tobe flew to my side saying, "Don, there's going to be some serious trouble here over that and you do not need to see it." He took me by the hand to find the shortest distance to the edge of a rather large playground and got me home, which wasn't very far.

I looked up to him and respected him. He was a good basketball player and a good student. He was also voted the best-looking boy for the High School Annual. I enjoyed his popularity with the girls. They learned very quickly that he was partial to me, so, I had several "older" girls being very sweet to me regularly. One of them followed him all the way to California when he found early work there, hoping to be able to be his choice for marriage. But Tobe had already picked Evelyn Harris, a sweet nice girl for his wife. He was soon back from California, and they were married.

Tobe soon joined the Air Force. WWII was raging and they needed radio gunners to ride those B-24's into Germany to do some strategic bombing. After several bombing missions, Tobe's plane was hit and had to limp over into Yugoslavia so they could bail out into high snow-covered mountains. He was 'missing in action' for 30 days during which the new Lucy Sinclair was born in Minden, Texas. Evelyn had moved to our home because some of her roads in the 'Jumbo' community were too slick to drive over when it rained. Our family took this grieving young daughter-in-law to the Henderson, Texas hospital to have her baby when her husband was 'missing in action.'

The pilot of Tobe's plane waited for the Navigator to tell him the plane was over 'friendly' territory, per their 'briefing' before they left England, so he could tell everyone to bail out. They were to walk a 4" steel guider out to the Bombay doors and jump into a pitch-black night into snow-covered mountains. Everyone wondered if they could do it. But when the man in front of Tobe balked, Tobe put his foot on his backside and they went out together. The fear of not getting a chance to jump outweighed the fear of jumping. The two pilots didn't make it. The plane was put into a circular pattern, but it struck one of the tall mountains before the Pilot and Co-Pilot could jump.

Morning came, but the Navigator didn't come down from his higher landing. Their training was for those lower down to stomp out a shelter in the snow and wait for those who landed higher to come down to them. They decided the Navigator was injured and climbed up to him. He wasn't wounded, but he could hear the guns of the front lines of the war, and he wasn't sure enough which side of that fighting they were on.

But he had figured it right, and the Yugoslavian soldiers came looking for survivors and brought them down safely. It took 28 days for Tobe to work his way around to England. His wife, Evelyn, and his baby girl, Lucy were really glad he was safe. Two more girls and one boy were born to Tobe and Evelyn. They and their two oldest girls died from lung cancer. The girls did not smoke, but Tobe and Evelyn were chain smokers, and the second-hand smoke always filled their home. A boy and a girl have continued to live in Minden, Louisiana. The girl has a grandson that would be about grown by now. I do not see them much at all. We just exchange Christmas cards. They seem to be doing well there.

I might make a note here that Minden, Texas, the place of mine and Tobe's birth, is a tiny little crossroad town that has lost its Post Office recently. Minden, Louisiana is a thriving city about 20 miles east from Shreveport, Louisiana. Tobe's work moved him there after WWII.

Tobe was one of my favorite people and was always telling me to come and see them in Minden, Louisiana. While I was trying to finish Theological Seminary, he said that over the phone. I promised him the first Thanksgiving after I finished school, I would be in his living room. We were watching the Army/Navy football game, and President John F. Kennedy was crossing over to show support to the other team for the second half. Tobe's son was about Jr. High School age, and he said, "Look, Dad! Our President is changing sides!" To which Tobe very quickly and angrily addressed his son's mistake with, "Son, that man is not OUR President. We will not allow that man to be OUR President!" It got very quiet, and I knew my "favorite person" was no longer my favorite person. He suffered a Louisiana viewpoint which disqualified him from being my friend.

Later, this 'distance' between Tobe and myself widened. I will tell this long story now to complete my sharing about Tobe. When mom became frail and needed more care, my father wanted to provide it in the little home he had bought 1 block from a huge grocery store in Henderson he could walk to. He even asked me what to do with his car, because he was not going to continue driving. He built a 'chinning' bar on the back porch to chin 3 times each morning in order to have the strength to put mom on the potty chair any time she said she wanted to go there, which was often. No one of the other children ever included me in any conversation about anything to do with family issues. They wanted to put mom in a nursing home where the care was complete day and night, etc. But none of them ever thought of including me in this discussion. I was still the 'baby.'

February and "Minister's Week" rolled around. Tobe had decided to go to Minden, Texas, and confront our father, Joseph, and take over this issue and get mom out of the house. He said he went into the house and told dad he was out of his mind trying to take care of mom there. About this they disagreed. But when Tobe told our father he was going to take over and get mom into a nursing home, our Dad went into his bedroom, reached under his pillow where he kept a .45 caliber automatic pistol Vance brought him as a gift from WWII, pointed it at Tobe and said, "There's the threshold to my house and you are never to come over it again or I will kill you!"

No one told me anything about this until I went to Minister's Week and Lennis immediately asked me what I thought about Papa Joe hitting Frankie. I froze in place because my father hated men who hit women. I picked up my suitcase and drove straight to their little home in Henderson. My father asked me through the screened door, "Which side are you on?" My moment of hesitation caused him to assume I had come to make trouble, too. He started for the bedroom where he kept the .45 pistol, and I quickly jerked the screen door open and rushed to catch him by the elbow to say, "Dad, nobody had even told me about this until I drove to Dallas where Lennis asked me about it. I immediately came here to you to find out what really happened."

He asked me if they told me that Frankie had slapped his face while he had my mother in his arms putting her on the potty chair. I said, no, they left that part out. He would not let the children even sass their mother. So, no child was to slap their father's face, ever! He placed my mother gently on her potty chair and kept turning to his right, so his left hand was cocked when he got back around to Frankie. He hit her with his fist and knocked her across the living room and she collapsed on the couch on the other side.

I explained that even though I agreed with the rest of the kids about what I would like to see him do with mom, I disagreed with them about whose decision that was. I assured him I believed it was his decision alone, and I would defend that right for him. My father knew he had only one friend in his family.

When Tobe told me about his visit, he said, "Don, that proves he's crazy and out of his head. He would have killed me with that gun!" My response was, "Tobe, that proves you are out of your head and crazy. He would have killed you, but that is what he would have done when he was 50, 60, or 70 years old. You don't just walk into a proud man's house who has responsibly brought 10 children through the worst depression the world has ever seen without anyone missing a meal and everyone who wanted to get an education got it, and tell him you are taking over. If he doesn't shoot you, there is something wrong with him."

That ripped it between me and Tobe. He went back to Minden, Louisiana and hand wrote me the meanest letter I have ever seen. It was on a yellow legal pad to give him room to write a long mean letter. I kept it for a while trying to decide whether it should be kept. I think I kept it, but I do not know where I filed it. Tobe & Evelyn are gone, and their two sweet oldest girls are gone. The younger two children do not need to see it, so, if I ever find it, I'll burn it.

James Dale Sinclair was Lula's and Joseph's next child. He was two years older than I was. We called him Dale at home. College and the military called him Jim. Dale had a lot of physical problems growing up. At the age of two, he fell into the big kitchen fireplace one winter playing where he should not have been playing. He had a long scar from his wrist bone to his elbow. When he was 13, he had 15 boils under the tough skin of that huge scar that had to be picked open. At 12 he developed an ulcer directly over the sight in his right eye. He had to drink canned carrot juice—terrible tasting stuff. He suffered a heart murmur by 17 years which kept him out of the Army for a while, but he finally was able to join and spent 2 years in Japan as Supply Sergeant with the occupation forces.

He was a good student. He earned a Batchelor's Degree in Chemistry at Stephen F. Austin College, but he didn't use it for a number of years. He took whatever job he could get and ended up working with a seismograph crew and insurance companies collecting small amounts on small policies. He met a girl in Crockett, Texas who wanted to marry him. I went down to Crockett and married him and the Sunday School Superintendent's daughter. That didn't turn out well.

The girl just wanted to get out from under her father's control and go honkey-tonking freely. Dale tried to cooperate with her, but he didn't like the drinking and wildness. So, they agreed to divorce. He showed me the charges she made against him. She accused him of dragging her all over the place with his work. They had actually been nowhere else except her father's free apartment he furnished them. I asked him if he planned on signing that accusation. He sheepishly said yes, that it was the best way to get it over with. He was always apologetic to me for having to divorce because I had married them.

He met another girl that wanted to marry him, and they had a retarded daughter. He, Dorothy, and their daughter, Brenda, began their lives together down close to Corpus Christie, Texas. Dale was collecting 25 to 50 cents a week on poor people's insurance policies. Every three months, he had to have his books checked and pay the company its money. He would call mom at Minden and ask for $450, but he was too embarrassed to tell her what it was for. After several times she pushed to find out what it was going for, she never did get a satisfactory answer. After mom's inheritance from her aunt ran out, she decided to tell me about that. It had gone on for five years. She said he would start crying and she was imagining the worst—drugs, alcohol, gambling, etc. She said she could just see a pistol up against his head while he was talking to her on the telephone. My proud father sat next to her saying, "You can bet your bottom dollar he's not getting any of my money like that!"

Men like to hear themselves say things like that. Sure enough, next stop over, he said, "Dale called again." I asked, "Did you send him the money?" He talked around that for a while but I kept asking it until he became angry and said, "What else can you do?" My response was, "Millions of things can be done about it if you just don't say—What else can you do?" I knew he would challenge that with, "Name one!" I said, "Send me the money and I will go down there, bail him out and report back to you exactly what it went for." "You would do that?" That was the quickest I had ever seen my father get over being angry. "Of course, I would do that! Better yet, call me and I will come by and get the money and head for Corpus. That would be quicker." We agreed that I would be prepared to move Dale's family to Minden to live while we figured what new directions they needed to go in.

So it went, and I was on my way—some 800 miles. I went a day earlier than expected so I could canvass the area to find out where Dale owed money and go to their home the next morning. I went in with my ultimatum. Dale had always loved me and thought I was something special. So, for me to unload on him about using all MY mother's money, etc. really was rough on him. I had brought a trailer to use in moving. Dorothy was to pack things up while Dale and I took the money around paying his debts. I brought in cardboard boxes, left the trailer, and we took off to spend the money.

Dale said, "Dorothy said she isn't going to Minden," I just whirled around and headed back to the house. He wanted to know where I was going. I said to get my trailer and go home. "What about the money?" "It goes with me. You can explain to your insurance company that you do not have their money—I think that's called 'fraud' in the business world." His response was, "Don, you scare me!" I knew it was working when he said that.

He went into the house and told Dorothy they had no choice but to go. She began to angrily pull things out to place in the trailer, and Dale and I went around distributing the money where it was needed. He was in none of the terrible trouble mom had imagined—he was just not making enough to support his family and used credit to get what they needed.

Leaving Corpus required we stop at the end of the block to get a friend to send their first grader's school records to Minden. While Dorothy was in the neighbor's house, he said, "Dorothy wants me to ask you if it is ok for her to smoke in your presence?" I said, "Sure, I just wish that was a big problem for us today."

They lived in Pasadena, Texas most of the time when Dale got a chemist's job mixing fertilizer on the ship channel. They lived there when the girl turned 18 years of age. Kathy and I were returning from a year in San Francisco and brought her a graduation present. When I carried it by, I noticed Dale had a different car. He always had trouble having a good car. It was parked off the street up beside the house. He told me a fast driver couldn't make the turn one night and rolled his car over and over up on top of Dale's car. He said the insurance man brought him a check for $1250.00. He told the insurance man he only paid $1150.00 for the wrecked car, and handed the $1250.00 back to the insurance man who got him a $1150.00 check.

I said in disbelief, "Dale, somewhere that insurance man sits in a coffee bar swapping stories with other agents. But when he tells that story no one believes it really happened." No insurance man has ever had that experience happen to them. It has never happened before and is not likely to happen again. But, that's my brother Dale. He did not want to cheat anyone or take advantage of anyone ever.

Dale developed Parkinson's disease, moved to a nursing home where he asked for a meeting with his wife, his retarded daughter, and his brother Don. He was worried that he had not completed making arrangements for his family's burial. I began checking out the possibilities. Dale had made one $87 payment on a burial plot with one of the commercial cemeteries many years before. I learned he could be buried in the Veteran's Cemetery in Houston for free. If they were cremated, his wife could be placed in the wall vault there with him if she did not remarry. And, their retarded daughter, Brenda, could be placed there if she did not marry and had no children. That part of the plan is not complete yet. They want to be sure Brenda has no children before they complete that part.

In the family meeting, Brenda suggested they plan on the Veteran's Cemetery and it was settled. Dale and Dorothy were placed there upon their death. Before the mother, Dorothy, died two amazing things happened. I discovered Dorothy was $40,000 in credit card debt and arranged for one of her checks to be used to pay down that huge debt—they were paying the "minimum" the companies recommended. She actually paid that off before she died.

After that was paid off, some royalties began to show up from our father, Joseph Sinclair's mineral rights purchases in Rusk County, which no one knew about. I again went to Dorothy and requested she set this money aside for her daughter's future after she died. They were leaving the girl penniless and unknown by any of the agencies and programs created for people like her. Dorothy readily agreed and asked me if I would handle this for Brenda. Dorothy prepared a will that stated Brenda, her daughter, was never to have control of any of this money. I thought that was a little tough, but I have learned it was important. Brenda can't handle numbers. How many days in a week, how many days in a month, I was able to use this to get her the support she needed.

Not long after that Dorothy broke her foot trying to squeeze through her bedroom door into her wheelchair. A surgeon had to make a hole completely through the foot to treat it. Dorothy had to go to a nursing home to recuperate further before completing his surgery. I was standing across her bed from a nurse working with her foot and fixing her bed. Dorothy kept crying and complaining saying, "Why can't I get my foot well? Other people's feet heal up! Why doesn't my foot get better?"

The nurse stepped up where she could look Dorothy squarely in the face and said, "Do you know who that is standing on the other side of this bed at 2:00 o'clock in the morning? It is your brother-in-law! I have never seen a brother-in-law standing by the bed of a sister-in-law in the middle of the night like this before! You should appreciate that he is even here!" That surprised both me and Dorothy, but it did calm Dorothy down some.

Dorothy had to return to the hospital early. I was standing in front of her room when the surgeon came in looking for her. I told him they had quickly moved her into isolation somewhere because she had developed a highly contagious disease. The surgeon left and soon returned to me saying, "She really has a very seriously contagious disease that will delay my completing the surgery." He left and I drove home.

Only a few days later, the hospital called to say she was being moved back to her room and the surgeon was going to complete his surgery in her room. I went back to Houston. The surgeon came in to do the surgery in her hospital room. He came out after completing the surgery and said, "I saw evidence of that highly contagious disease still in her foot during my surgery. I just hope she can recover from both my surgery and that disease at the same time." He told me she would not wake up for hours, so I drove back to Coldspring, getting home about 10:00 PM. At 3:30 AM, the hospital called to say Dorothy had died in her room. I had her body cremated and placed in the Veteran's Cemetery Wall with Dale's.

I had to take Brenda all around to the organizations and agencies that were created for persons in her condition and prove to them she was qualified for their programs. I learned to wait for the people to question Brenda and turn to me questioning why I thought she was qualified for their programs.

I would prove this to them by telling them to ask Brenda when she was born. "When were you born?" "56!" The staff member would look back at me with a questioning look. I would say, "Ask her how old she is." "How old are you?" "56!" At this point, staff began to understand that their tests do not catch some conditions of some people they should help. I used this test over and over and over.

One humorous moment came when the Mental Health people wanted to include Brenda so much, they gave their test the 2nd time—they resisted this so strongly that I suspect it has never been done before or since. Brenda's IQ bounces around in the '80s. After they gave her the test the second time Brenda said to me, "Uncle Don, I tried as hard as I could on that test." When I explained that the better a person does on that test the more unqualified, they are. Brenda said, "You mean I was hurting myself the better I did on that test?" I laughed and told her that the good news is that she flunked it again. She scored in the upper 80s and 80 is the mark above which the Mental Health programs cannot serve you. The Mental Health people wanted to help Brenda so badly, but they just couldn't because she was just a little too bright. She was proud. We had a good laugh and went on to the next agency.

We finally put together enough for Brenda to have a little money. She wanted to live alone in Houston, but we tried several places that did not work out. After the 911 firemen had to kick her door in three times to get her up out of her chair to get to the bathroom, we began looking for a nursing home she could live in. We found Bradford on the Avon in Livingston, Texas—15 miles from my home in Coldspring, Texas. They took her on trial, but it worked out really well. They were able to keep her using what money we had garnered for her to live on. She has been there for over 10 years and is doing fine. The extra checks from Joseph Sinclair's royalty investments are now smaller than at first—$100 here and $200 there—but I use it for special things Brenda needs. She got a new "tablet" from it last year and a new rolling walker recently. She is planning for a new "computer" for Christmas.

THAT BRINGS US TO THE LAST CHILD OF JOSEPH & LULA KATE!

Donald Wood Sinclair was born October 6, 1929—the same month of the worst global depression the world has ever seen and the same month of Lula Kate's father's death. That was the month Joseph paid Lula Kate's family for their part of my grandfather's big house on the hill above Minden, Texas, and we moved in. I was raised in that splendid 2-story house with hand-planed lumber, 5 fireplaces and surrounded by long covered porches with banisters. I never discovered I was "upper crust" because my parents never acted that way to other people. They both had extreme integrity and were both highly respected by everyone I ever met. I thought everyone was supposed to be that way.

One privilege I had that none of my siblings had was to have Lula Kate at home alone while the older children were in school. I was able to ask her about anything and everything. She was the greatest mother a child could have. And her father was Minden's Walmart—a huge 2-story store located at the crossroads that created the little town of Minden, Texas. She had the key and I got to go into that huge store with her, so she could give some poor child shoes and clothes left after her father died.

Joseph stopped farming the year I was born, but he kept his farm and taught us to raise food which was what kept us, our kinfolks, and our neighbors from getting hungry during the great depression of the 1930s. Everybody would come to consult with my father about everything. I was sure he was one of the wisest men in the world.

The poor, especially, came to seek his advice. Without cars, they would walk long distances at night just to ask his advice. Timey, the washwoman every Monday, walked 3 miles at night to consult with him. I wanted to hear what she came for, so I moved close enough I could hear them talking. She said 2 white men had come to her house to say there was going to be a new road built through her area that would take out her house and the 12 acres her husband had left her. My father told her there was no road to be built near her place and that the men were just trying to get her property for themselves. As Timey thanked him and turned to walk back home, Joseph said to her, "Timey, if those white men ask you who told you, I wish you would tell them Joe Sinclair called them liars." She thanked him and disappeared into the darkness armed with the truth of a white man she knew and trusted. He hated people who tried to take advantage of the poor.

But I couldn't understand why my family could not agree to treat blacks as equals. My father loved and hunted with a huge black man his age because he had the best hunting dogs around. He had a 5-year-old son when I was 5, and we became very close friends. I was playing basketball with Sammy Tatum in 1934 east Texas when I expressed excitement about starting school. Sammy said he was not going to school. I picked up the basketball to ask Sammy, "Why?" He said something I have never recovered from, "I ain't got no school to go to."

That night at the dinner table, that 5-year-old white boy, sitting on his feet so he could reach the table, asked a father who was on the School Board for 30 years, "Daddy, is it true Sammy does not have a school to go to?" My father said, "Yes, I am sorry to say that is true." The other five people around that table slowly went back to eating. I haven't eaten since.

Timey came over every Monday to help my mother wash—black pot with fire under it, number 3 washtub, rubbing board—every Monday. My mother and I would eat lunch together, then she would go to the door and say, "Timey, you can come in and eat now." I asked my mother why she did that. She placed me behind the door, so I could observe Timey eating. After seeing Timey eat with her hands and slurping food off bread rather than using a fork or a spoon, my mother quietly closed the door and moved back to her ironing without a word. I looked at her and thought, "She thinks she answered my question." I wanted to ask why we didn't teach Timey to use a fork or spoon, but I decided that would not settle the issue.

What was happening to me was I was confronting RACISM. My young mind was not able to understand it, but I did begin to feel the pain of it and to understand that there was something seriously wrong with the world I lived in, and my own wonderful family was part of it. What I knew at 5, I still know at 90. There is a better way, and I always fight for it.

Another humorous story that happened around that washing team. The first thing you do when washing a kid's overalls is to reach into the front pockets and turn the pockets wrong side out where the dirt is. My mother pulled one of my pockets out like that and had a handful of cigarette grounds in her hand. I had picked up a "ready roll" cigarette butt to find out what it was like to smoke. My mother got a huge #3 washtub, filled it full of purple hull peas, and made me sit there and shell that large tub of purple hull peas as punishment. The real truth is that I had no interest in smoking after trying it one time, but, from that day on, if anyone offered me a cigarette to smoke, it looked a lot like a purple hull pea, and nobody ever had a desire to smoke a purple hull pea.

More importantly, my mother initiated my ability to study or read people. The old cars had room for a child to stand on the front floorboard on the passenger side. When my mother went to the big city with my dad, that's where I stood. My dad would park facing the busy sidewalks and as people walked by my mother would say, "That man is sad about something not going right for him." "That lady seems happy and is probably bringing good news home to her family." "I wonder why that man is walking so slowly. He seems to be worried about what will happen where he is going."

I would stand there looking at people and being coached by my mother about what was going on in their lives. I now have a lecture that contains four of the times I have pushed into individual's lives about serious things to prove they aren't being honest with themselves or others about what is going on in their lives. I have become so capable at this that I hesitate to ever do it, but I often know more about a person than they know about themselves.

The last paragraph of that lecture has a statement saying that I am aware that saying I know more about another person than they know about themselves is the most arrogant and egotistical claim a person can make. I guess I could blame my mother because she started the whole thing.

At 12 years old, I visited my mother's sister's home for a weekend. She had some great kids, but her biscuits were not cooked long enough. We went to their Church on Sunday. I wasn't paying much attention until the Preacher shouted out that those "Priests keep those Nuns in those convents just for their pleasure!" I thought how horrible! It looks like someone would have stopped it. I knew very little about the Roman Catholic Church except it had been around a long, long time. Then I thought Robin Hood would have stopped that! Then I thought the Sheriff of Nottingham wasn't that bad of a guy. He would have stopped it! My next thought made me a revolutionary, "That Preacher is lying! What he is saying is not true!" I began to look around to see if God had revealed to others what God had just revealed to me. I couldn't find any one of the 40 people present who had received the revelation I had. But without any knowledge or proof, I became clear that that Preacher was lying. And, I knew I was right!

At 12, I began to seriously read the Bible. When I came to Adam's rib, I took it to my mother. She said, "Sure, that's true son. That's why all men have a rib missing on one side." I was impressed with this book. But in a class at school, we had to bring current events each Monday taken from magazines or newspaper. One person brought a news story about a road crew scooping up a skeleton in a shallow grave. The sheriff investigating said his first problem was to figure out if it was a skeleton of a man or a woman. My hand just raised itself to answer that question. When the teacher asked for my recommendation I said, "Just count the ribs. If there is a rib missing it is a male skeleton, because God took a rib out of Adam to create Eve."

Everybody just roared with laughter. For the rest of the year, they always greeted me with, "How many ribs do you have now, Sinclair?" They thought their teasing bothered me, but what really bothered me most was how many other things has my mother taught me that are not true! Since that time, I have developed as many analytical abilities as I could to defend against making such mistakes. I do not like things that are not true but I love things that are true!

At 14 and 15, I would sit in Church (as the only young person present) and listen to the adults discuss God, the Bible, and current events. My thoughts were that if the Christian Faith meant what we say it does and the German

Christians let the Christian Faith mean that much to them, we would not be having this horrid WWII that was going on. German Christian mothers and American and English Christian mothers were sending their Christian sons out to kill other Christian sons? I resolved that neither side really believed what they say they believe or we would not be having this war.

My father had 5 sons in WWII. I am glad they all got home safely, but nothing has changed about the faith issue. We are all back to being the 'somewhat' Christians we think we should be, but I know it is not the real Christian Faith which is powerful and loving and does not tolerate exceptions.

Because of this "gift" of early insight, I often find myself at odds with the public understanding of issues. My mother was most aware of this. When I was 19 years old, home from three years in the Air Force and waiting for college sessions to start, we were in the kitchen alone again. Taking food out of her oven she asked me, "Do you remember asking your father about Sammy's school?" I said, "Like it was yesterday, mom." She said, "Well, I thought you had been carrying that around all these years. I want to tell you something about your father. Every year, when the School Board begins its planning, your father pulls out the papers that state their responsibility. He reads it out loud, 'We are charged with furnishing educational opportunities for ALL the youth in our School District!'" Mom said the rest of the School Board gets angry with him for doing that, but he reads it to them every year. He knows they aren't going to spend any of that money on the black children but he wants them to know they are leaving some kids out. I was glad she shared that with me. It helped me with my relationship with my father for the rest of his life.

On the Sunday before Christmas, my father would come home with a car trunk filled with apples, oranges, grapefruit, candy, etc. Our family would go with him to the "colored" section homes. My father would ask, "How many children do you have in your home?" We would fill that many paper bags with enough for each child to have something for Christmas and give it to the families.

On that Sunday, a few years later, my father stopped in front of a small white building sitting in a cotton patch. He said to me, "That's Sammy's school, but Sammy's father is a sharecropper and needs Sammy to help prepare and plant the seeds in the soil, and he has to have Sammy help harvest each crop later. That means Sammy cannot come to school except for about 3 months. We keep a teacher there for those 3 months each year." The small building looked so empty and deserted. There was no beaten path around it or playground equipment. I looked at that building out the back window as my father drove away, and it faded in the distance.

Lula Kate's health failed first and Joseph bought a small house in Henderson one block from a large grocery store. Once it became clear my father was going to take care of Lula Kate himself Syble and Bear bought a house next to them. Syble was really great to come over every day to prepare food for them. Frankie also would come from across town to help out. Joseph told me they were both always hollering at him, especially when he was picking Lula Kate up and placing her on the potty chair he had bought.

My father and I planned together some serious things he wanted to do that none of the others in the family would have supported him in. And, at one point he felt so bad about his kids he said to me, "Sometimes I wish I had no kids at all!" I couldn't let him deny his own greatness, so I said, "Let me tell you about your youngest child." I recounted some of my major accomplishments and ended with, "Dad, I have so many wonderful and creative friends in this world that you could drop me out of a plane over any continent except China or Russia and by night I would be in the home of friends." He listened and looked at me as though he couldn't believe it but had to and said, "Well, that's enough to make a father proud!"

I must share the last few serious things we planned without the rest of the family involved. When Joe Sinclair and Lula Kate Evens Welch married, they each had a gravesite planned beside their first marriage partners. They had one short discussion about that. "We will each be buried beside our first marriage partners." In 50 years, they had not discussed that issue again. In spite of the fact that my father had purchased three gravesites to place their daughter Lucy on one side of and had a small cement wall raised around it, their original plan 50 years earlier was followed when my mother was buried. Mom's body was placed beside her first marriage partner.

It was months later he was shocked that he hadn't remembered Lucy's gravesite prepared with three graves. He called me about it and said he needed to correct this and move mom's grave up there with Lucy's grave and he would be buried in the third site on the end. I readily agreed with him that had they ever talked about that mom would rather be buried beside Lucy than anywhere else in the world.

He reminded me that the rest of his family would really come after him for being out of his head again, with which I readily agreed, but I had a plan to head them off. He was to go to the family lawyer, Rayford Shaw, to learn what the law says about moving graves, and then go to the cemetery committee to check the rules there. Then he could freely move mom's grave up there. When the family came after him, he was just to take them to let the lawyer inform the family about the law. Which was, "Mr. Sinclair can move Mrs. Sinclair's grave every day of the year as long as he owns the grave site, he puts her in."

Then all hell broke loose. The older girls in his family created the accusation that their father was so jealous of his wives he could not stand for mom to be down there with her first marriage partner. Then I took one of mom's letter-writing tablets out of the small drawer she kept them in and told my father while the sisters were finishing food preparation and could hear us, "Use this tablet to do two things: 1) Draw some shapes you think the headstone should have. Create several of them because when the person who makes headstones asks, 'what shape stone do you want?' your mind always goes blank. And 2) use another page to write what words you want on the headstone. Do this several times, too, because that's harder than the shape of the stone. Then we'll go shopping with this preparation and order a headstone."

Hearing this the older girls began to realize how our father was so ready for them to scream at him about moving the grave in the first place. "YOU HAVE BEEN WORKING WITH HIM ALL ALONG HAVEN'T YOU!!!" My simple response was, "Of course."

They didn't let up. Every time I stopped by and they were in the house they would say, "Don, he hasn't mentioned that tablet work you planned with him. He's out of his head and has forgotten all about your planning!" Every time, the minute they left and got out of the yard, that disciplined father of mine would pull out that little drawer and we would pick up our planning right where we left it off. He was just done discussing anything with them. But I could not tell them this.

Soon after this, my father suffered Gout in his big toe so bad, they had to take him to the hospital. Several members of his family were there on the Sunday afternoon I was able to be there. The rest of the family seemed so eager to prove he was out of his head, so when he told me that Gout was a mixture of infection and arthritis and often started in the big toe, I figured I had another way to check if he is out of his head or not. It was Sunday, but his doctor came into the room. I moved back out into the hall because I wanted to check with his doctor about what Gout was like. I got the chance when his doctor came out of the room. I asked him about Gout, and he gave me the same description my father had given me. I knew he still wasn't out of his head.

One of the older sisters told me the tombstone had been placed at the graves, and they would take him by to see it on Tuesday when they released him from the hospital. I felt like things were coming to an end for Joseph Jarrell Sinclair, because that tombstone was the last thing on his list to do, "And I'm done!" That's the way he put it to me when we began planning how he would do those "last things." I made a point that day of squeezing his hand, looking him squarely in the eyes, and in front of the whole family that was standing there, "I want to thank you for all you have done for all of us here!" His hand squeezed mine as we just looked into each other's faces. And I left. That was the last time I saw him alive.

Tuesday, they took him home. On the way, they took him by the cemetery to see the headstone. Wednesday morning, he got out of bed and went to his quilt-covered rocking chair in front of his TV, and sat down without turning the TV on. The sisters said it was strange. He didn't want to eat anything, drink anything, and had no pain anywhere in his body. They took him to the hospital about 11:30 PM, and the doctor said the same thing. "Mr. Sinclair is not sick, he has no pain, he's a little dehydrated, and he's dying when there's nothing wrong with him." He was dead by 3:30 AM. I was living in the Dallas Religious House—some of those 'friends' I had told him about—and the head Prior David and I were headed for West Texas to keep appointments that would change the world a little more for the better. Dallas knew our schedule, and the telephone came in ahead of us in Sweetwater, Texas—our next appointment.

I left my station wagon with Prior David and caught a bus back to Dallas to get with Kathy and we traveled to Minden, Texas one more time to bury Joseph Jarrell Sinclair in front of that headstone for him and his second marriage partner. If you are ever in Maple Grove Cemetery in Minden, Texas look what he put on that tombstone. Joseph lived almost 90 years and gave it all to his family and the community of Minden. He was NEVER out of his head at any time!

When my father died, I was the only friend he had in his own family and he knew that. I had defended his right to make those basic decisions even when everyone else in the family wanted to take over what little rights he had left. So, the little 'runt' tagging along at the end of the family chain, who was never given credit for understanding things well enough to participate in decisions, had more normal good sense than all the others put together. He knew that, too!

To prepare for my work as Pastor to United Methodist Churches I went to school for 8 years plus another 4 years to gain the Dr. of Ministry degree. This education was delayed because all the colleges and universities were filled to capacity with all the GI's returning home from WWII. I couldn't get a chair in any classroom in 1946.

So, I was only 16 years old. I just waited until I turned 17 on October 6th and joined the Air Force. They promised me I would be sent to Europe rather than Asia. But once you take the oath to serve you have to go where they send you. So, after 8 weeks of teletype school in Scott Field near Chicago, where I helped accuse our commanding officer of crimes and got him kicked out of the Air Force, I was sent to help man Nichols Airfield in Manila, Philippine Islands until we turned that over to the civil authorities. We were moved 60 miles north to Clark Airfield where I spent the remainder of my time of 2 years overseas.

Most of the men in the service chased after the women readily available around the airbase. The Philippine Islands had 2 big wars in WWII. One when the Japanese came through with many troops and a lot of firepower and control of the air and the water. They really blasted all the buildings and bridges and killed a lot of the people—especially the fighting men. Then, four years later, here comes General McArthur up from Australia and New Guinea with more firepower and men to burn and blow up everything to dislodge the well-entrenched Japanese. The Philippine Islands were torn to shreds both times.

So, the women were left to make the best they could out of a very bad situation. I just could not bring myself to take advantage of them. For $25 per month, you could have your own girlfriend with her own raised-up bamboo hut, and you could spend any night there you wanted to. Many soldiers would sneak up to 'their' hut just to check on their girlfriend, but nobody ever caught their girlfriend with another guy. I was amazed! But those women dreamed that the soldier would take her back to The United States with them. They wouldn't dare damage that chance by having another man around.

I spent my time with the Chaplain's Assistant. I had a clear tenor voice and loved singing in the chapel services. Then, at 3:00 PM every Sunday, the Methodist youth meetings were held all over Luzon Island. We would carry a small pump organ in a weapons carrier, and drive out miles to different youth meetings and help the Pastors. I met one of those youth leaders who came to the Seminary in Dallas years later.

I was surprised to see so many Baptist missionaries but only one silver-haired woman Methodist missionary. We would take our organ into a small prison for white-collar criminals and go with her and make music. It came clear to me that The Methodist Church needed to put more people into these islands. I had a simple formula for deciding what to do with your life. If you see a big need and you are in a position to do something about it—that was God's way of calling you to do just that. I planned to come home, get the training I would need, and return to serve this mission field. That was clear as a bell.

When it came time to come home, I was going around checking out with the Laundry, library, etc. to guarantee all was clear, and finally to headquarters to finish up. My commanding officer was there when the master sergeant was checking me out. I knew he was being pressured by Wing Headquarters in Tokyo to get some of his experienced teletype operators to stay with him an extra 4 months rather than going home early. There were 12 operators in his crew. I was one of the two best operators he had, but the other 11 operators all received promotions to Staff Sergeant the month before. Some of those 11 were 'goof offs', even had been court-martialed for not showing up for duty.

So, my commanding officer was not ready for the anger I had toward him when he said, "Sergeant, are you homesick?" "No, sir. I don't get homesick!" "Do you have a girlfriend waiting for you when you get home?" "No, Sir, I do not!" "Well, you might be interested in giving up your 4 months back home and just staying with us here." "No, sir. I wouldn't be interested in staying here any longer than absolutely necessary!" "Sergeant, are you getting smart with me? Do you just not like the way I run this outfit?" "Yes, sir. I do not like the way you run this place! I'm getting out of here as fast as I can!"

At this, the master sergeant turned away from the filing cabinets where records were kept and said, "Sir, I just might have a clue in my hand as to why Sergeant Sinclair wants to leave us so bad. Sergeant, why didn't you get promoted last month along with all the other men?" "That's my question, let the commanding officer answer it! There is no reason! I'm one of two best operators he has and the promotion was there to give!"

The commanding officer took the page, checked with the master sergeant if there was any reason. Finding none he turned back to me. "Sergeant if you do go home now you will not get that promotion back there. I will make you a deal, if you will stay with us, I will see personally that you get that promotion next month." My response was, "You are asking me to trust you with 4 months of my life because if you didn't make it work, I would just be staying on here when I could be back there mustering out." "Yes, sergeant, that's true, and I don't blame you for being ticked off with me. This shouldn't have happened. But I want you to get the promotion you have earned. Let's say if I don't get you that promotion within the first month, I will promise you I will break every rule in the book to get you back home, which you also deserve." He stuck out his hand, and, it's not a valid deal to make with any military officer, but we shook hands.

It was December. The commanding officer began to come by our teletype station every day to see if the promotion had come in. He also began to come to the chapel services to hear me sing. Just before Christmas, he expressed dismay and asked me if I were ready to go home. I reminded him that Wing Headquarters was operating in Tokyo on ½ staff because of vacations there, and everything is going to be late. Two days later, the promotion came through our teletype system. He was thrilled as was I. We became very good friends for the next four months, and I went to Carswell Air Force Base in Ft. Worth for a short stay and was discharged from there as a Staff Sergeant in 1949.

It was January 1950 when my studies for the ministry started at Lon Morris College in Jacksonville, Texas. The first night on campus, a group of about 10 decided we would walk the 3 blocks to the First Methodist Church's evening service. When we walked into the sanctuary, one of the groups was picking the row and ushered us all into the pew where we would sit for the service. When I came up to her, she ushered me in and followed behind rather than wait for the others. What I didn't know was that she was picking me to sit with her because she was graduating in 3 months, and I was the interesting new guy on campus.

After the church service, all of us went to Saddlers' restaurant for refreshments. I found myself sitting at the same small table with her. After the others had all gone back to the college, she called attention to the fact that her curfew was in 10 minutes and we had to hurry back to campus or she would be in a little trouble. So, I called a cab and delivered her on time. That proved to be the only time in the history of that small college a student had brought a girl home in a cab.

Unaware of this, when I went to breakfast in the basement dining room of my dorm, there was a large group of students sitting at one table with one empty chair 'turned up.' I was encouraged to take that chair that Katherine

Carter had reserved for me. It took me a little while to realize that the entire student body was assigning me to be Kathy's boyfriend, which was all right with me. We liked each other, and I had a new electric typewriter and typed 80 words per minute. She liked handing me her handwritten papers to type overnight for her. She pretended she liked to sit and watch me practice the piano lessons I had always wanted to have a chance to do. Hence, I entered Lon Morris in January 1950. By August 27, 1950, we were married at the altar of Grace Methodist Church in Houston, Texas—70 years ago August 27, 2020 at the close of morning worship. We still have the iron skillet Mr. Houston gave to Kathy on that day.

So, I was married, received my first Pastor's assignment, and bought my first automobile all within the same week. Kathy and I were on our way for 46 years of appointments in The Texas Annual Conference of The United Methodist Church.

For several years I served as Pastor of small churches close to schools I would be attending or Associate Pastor in larger multiple clergy churches which were in the city where the university was located. When I met with the Board of Missions after arriving at Perkins School of Theology in Dallas, I learned that the reason I saw no Methodist missionaries in the Philippine Islands was because the mission had already raised up native Pastors. The plan was not to stay on and 'run' things but just provide the Philippine Pastors what specialists they needed. All eight of those 'specialist' positions were filled. By then we were very entrenched in The Texas Annual Conference with headquarters in Houston. I have found it to be as much a mission field as the Philippine Islands would have been.

I will refrain from telling most of the interesting events during those 46 years, but I will share some of the more important ones. I developed parish-related programs in each church I served. My belief was that each congregation was responsible for the geographical location where it was located. The people humorously named it "The TV Guide" of our ministry. In it was serious events planned to minister to all the people who lived in that Parish.

My work attracted the attention of the conference staff in the Methodist Board of Education. The head of that Staff wanted me to develop that approach from the Conference-Wide position of Adult Work, which soon got changed to Adult Training.

Kathy and I were also beginning a 21-year experiment to create materials in helping families in the church have materials on how to raise children with an 18-year plan for each child. At the same time, I discovered that 8 clergy families of Seminary graduates and their professor, Joseph Mathews, had established this type of advanced experiment on how to restore the 'humaneness' in the worst community they could find in Chicago, Illinois. I knew that professor and most of those graduates. I established a relationship with their programming, and Kathy and I sent each of our 4 sons to their special Academy immediately upon graduating High School.

Our whole family attended their "Summer Assembly" each July for years because of their great work renewing that "5th City" community. It was The Church being The Church as I understood it should be. My local work was tied in with their type of work. I recruited persons to work with them and they provided me with leadership in Texas and the South.

One of the humorous things that happened to our family while attending the July Summer Assembly for 500 Christians from across the globe was when Joseph Mathews thought the groups doing analysis and planning were working too hard from daylight to dark. He asked for small singing groups to form, rehearse, and go bursting into these planning groups singing. Three of our sons and I located a girl named Barbara, changed her name to Grace so we could call our singing group "Four Sins and a Grace". "Fiddler on The Roof" was a popular movie that year. It had a beautiful song in it sung by a poor farmer whose daughters wanted to decide who they married. It began, "Is this the little girl I carried?..." We burst into one of the workgroups unannounced and began our song. The woman standing at the chalkboard writing down the ideas their group was making collapsed and fell to the floor. We continued our song as several went to tend to the lady on the floor. Afterward, I stepped over to where she was sitting to say, "I know we are not the best singers in the world, but I didn't think we were that bad!" She said, "You don't understand. I left my six week old baby with my mother in England to come to this Summer Assembly and I have been missing her so much. Then your group popped in singing that song. The combination just caused me to faint."

Mine and Kathy's most tragic year was 1979, with the loss of our 4th son, Stanley. When he was in high school a fellow student chose him to tell about her father having sex with her since she was 7 years old. She said she was beginning to realize that was not supposed to happen to her daughters. Stanley talked her into consulting with me about what she needed to do about this. She was surprised to learn Stanley had not told me about it already. I assured her Stanley realized the seriousness of this and would never have told me if she had not agreed to talk with me about it. He knew it was her very serious situation and he would never share it with anyone unless she gave him permission.

Her big question to me was, "Will my mother get into trouble if I tell the authorities?" I told her I would have to check with the District Attorney on that. He said if she knew and did nothing about it, she would be considered as guilty as the father. The girl decided she would not report this crime because she did not want to get her mother in trouble. She was planning on running away to a large city to get away from her father. I asked her what she would do if her father raped other girls. She said she could not stand for that and would accuse her father. I told her it probably would happen again, so she might be making this decision all over again. She ran away to a large city.

Within six months, her father raped two young sisters—9 and 11 years old. The daughter came home immediately to report her father's treatment of her, and he was arrested. His mother bailed him out immediately. Our son had moved on to college at the University of Houston and had started a rock band there. They won a USO contest and were sent to entertain troops all around the Mediterranean Sea.

After returning to Houston, he got a job reading meters for the power company. He always parked his car in a free parking area and walked several blocks to work. After work, as he walked up to his car while Kathy was waiting to have dinner with him during her Christmas/New Year's holiday time, two people in jogging suits jogged up to him. One held his arms back while the other one stuck a professional knife into his heart, and they jogged on. We know this because a lady saw it from a distance and told the police how it happened. The police were three blocks away and were there within 15 minutes, but Stanley was already dead.

The police investigators called me 300 miles north of Houston to tell me it was a "murder for hire" situation. Someone had paid money to get professionals to kill my son. They also asked me if we knew Stanley was gay, and I said, "No." We were dumbfounded by all this, but the daughter in the incest case came to our home to tell us she believed her father had arranged Stanley's death because Stanley had broken up his "playhouse."

Kathy and I were coming to the same conclusion because no one else had hated our son enough to do this. My mind went immediately to my own safety because I was also involved in his being held accountable and had talked with the girl several months earlier than his alibi would allow. I knew the father personally and was sure the daughter was right. He hated religion and my ability to read people kicked in. I went to all the authorities, Sheriff, Police Chief, Mayor, and District Attorney to request permission to carry a pistol to defend myself. They all refused, but I told them all he would come after me some Sunday during the worship service. I even told them which door of the church building he would use and made plans to escape and draw him out the back door to keep him from the congregation. I told all of them that he had to do something radical to keep from going to court where a judge could tell him to shut up and sit down. I told them he would do this before the trial to interrupt the trial. He could not tolerate having people judge or criticize him. But he wanted me because I had judged him and participated in his downfall.

I talked with my District Superintendent about it, and we decided I would be moved to another church in Houston. We would publish the move on the front page of the local newspaper so everyone would know I was not in that church anymore.

I had just told my new congregation in Houston that I would go to his trial that had been moved to another city. The District Attorney had asked me to come to the trial to sit with the daughter whose mother refused to support her.

But, on June 10, 1980, two weeks after I had been moved, my phone rang just after the worship service. The call was from a lady in the town and church I had been moved from. She reported that this father had gone into the Baptist Church with two rifles, one .45 caliber pistol, and one .22 caliber pistol, kicked his way through the swinging doors into the sanctuary, and began to shoot people standing singing a hymn.

Behind the swinging door on the shooter's left was the church's new speaker system controls, and an experienced man was showing a young man about 25 years old how to run their new equipment. That young man, who had been a student of the shooter 12 years earlier, saw only the barrel of the rifle and grabbed it. The shooter tried to shake him off his rifle and finally threw the rifle and the young man into the floor of the church, grabbed for his second rifle hooked over his shoulder. That rifle had a new belt on it, and the scuffling had caused the buckle to come loose and the rifle fell to the floor behind him. He then pulled out the .45 caliber pistol and tried to shoot the young man. The young man dodged back and forth and finally jumped into the stairs that led to the basement without being shot.

By this time a 250 lb. man charged him driving him into the foyer of the church. The shooter killed that man with the .45 caliber pistol. By then another man charged the shooter as he was crawling from under the first man and drove him out of the church into the yard. The shooter also killed that man with his .45 caliber pistol. All he had left was the .22 caliber pistol and he had lost his thick glasses. He crawled from under the second man and tried to run to his left, stumbled into the street, got up, and stumbled over the second curb. His .22 caliber pistol accidentally discharged striking the shooter across his own forehead. That's where the police found him unconscious.

Instead of going to a trial that was to begin the next day, I went back to the town where the shooting happened. The city Mayor and I had become very close friends over his grandson's death while I was there. When he spotted me, he told me to go wait in his courtroom. He was going to assemble all the lawmen in town to have a conversation with me about this incident. He brought in over 20 lawmen including the FBI agents and 2 game wardens and told them he was going to start a conversation with me. They were to join in at any time they had a question.

The Mayor's first question was, "Why did he go to the Baptist Church? You told us he would come into the Methodist church!" I answered that he knew I was not in the Methodist Church, but he hated all religions equally. I described his thinking that the Methodist Church had large doors of 2X6 inch lumber and strong brass fittings. He could not kick his way through them, and he was in no mood to do the backing up you have to do to open those heavy doors. The Baptist Church had not replaced their sanctuary yet, and he could kick his way through their doors, which he did shouting, "This is war!"

I then asked the Police Chief how many rounds of ammunition he had. The Chief said, "450 rounds." I said, "There weren't that many Baptists in that service. I then asked him where he parked his car. The Chief said he had parked up at the corner of the courthouse square between the two churches. Then the Chief said, "You think he was going to both churches!" I said I was certain of that.

The shooter's first bullet fired as he swept his gun from right to left, hit an 8-year girl in the head killing her instantly. Her father had just been hired to lead the choir in the United Methodist Church. That mother had to run across the courthouse square and run shouting into the Methodist Church, "Our daughter has just been killed by a gunman in the Church." This congregation closed down its worship service and ran across the courthouse square to help people caught in this horrible situation.

The shooter was sent to John Sealy Hospital in Galveston, Texas to heal from his wound. He was brought back periodically to ask, "Is he capable of helping his lawyer in his trial?" After several times finally, the answer was "Yes," so the authorities kept him in the special suicide-proof cell the Mayor had built for him at the Mayor's own expense, "so they will not take that son-of-a-bitch away from us!" The trial was to begin the next Monday.

Again, my phone rang the Sunday before the trial. The same lady had called to say, "The world is a safer place today. They have just found the shooter had hung himself in a suicide proof cell." He had torn his towel into 1-inch strips, fastened it to the low door of his special cell, reached down to pull both of his feet up off the floor with his hands, and held them up until he was dead.

The Mayor in the story above and I had become very special friends over his grandson's car accident death and our son's murder. They happened about the same time, and the Mayor had come by my office weeping over his grandson's death, saying, "You and your wife seemed to be handling it and going on with your lives. I'm dying over this grandson. I go to the cemetery every day and just sit and look at his grave. I want to know what you and your wife did to manage the pain and sorrow after your son's death."

I gave him some psychological possibilities of why it was harder on him. He owned half the county, a small train to move steel products produced by the steel mill, which he also owned. I suggested he was always the boss wherever he went. I, on the other hand, owned very little and was not in charge everywhere I went. He rejected such psychological reasons, and he kept saying, "What did you do? What did you say to your family?" I finally told him we held a family meeting like we had done every Sunday afternoon for 20 years. "What did you say to your family?" I said we told ourselves that we would each have to come to the time when we could let go of Stanley. That it might happen soon and suddenly, or it may be weeks and months. But they were to allow their feelings to run their course and not try to hide the sorrow. Then we review our son's life briefly describing what we especially remembered about him. At the end, I proposed that if we had a book representing Stanley's life what title would we put on the book?

Our oldest son often sensed such values and could find words to express them better than the rest of us. After a silence, he said, "It's been 19 glorious years!" That satisfied everyone in the family, and we were ready to adjourn and go back to our own lives.

The Mayor jumped up, stepped up to hug me, and said, "That will do it for me too! I have been letting my pain and loss be the big thing rather than appreciate the life my grandson did have. "It's been 18 glorious years." We became very close friends after that.

In 1965, one of my closest clergy friends, Dr. Bill Scales, called to say Dr. Martin Luther King, Jr. had arrived at the outskirts of Montgomery, Alabama after the 50-mile walk from the Selma, Alabama bridge incidents. He put out a call to all those who sympathized with what he was doing to come to a small church 3 miles outside Montgomery to create a mass of people on his march into Montgomery. Four of us drove all night to get there to join the marchers.

They arranged us curb to curb for a mile with men on the sides in case there were some bricks or cans thrown at us. As we entered the city that mass of people turned right down a street off the main street into town. After we turned back left, I realized why Dr. King mapped out this route. We were in the black community of the city, and he wanted those people to see those 50 thousand marchers who agreed with them in their struggle for equal rights. I saw one elderly black woman sitting in a rocking chair on her front porch slowly clapping her hands together and saying, "Ain't nothing can stop all them people!"

After the program and speakers were done, we all had to make our own way back to our cars parked 3 miles away. Our four stopped at a fast-food place in the black community. It had three service windows and a large crowd of black marchers lined up at each one. I was the first of our four white persons to step up to the service window. I said, "Where are your windows for the white folks?" It got suddenly quiet and still until the crowd realized it was a friendly joke. Laughter broke out across the hundreds of people in that crowd. My best friend said, "Sinclair, you are going to get us killed!" My response was, "Not in this crowd. These are OUR people!"

We were warned about driving home that some of these white people would be out to kill us. Our trip was uneventful, but Mrs. Luizo had come to Alabama to help the marchers. There were 300 of them that made the complete march and they needed a ride back to Selma. I think she was a cab driver's wife from Pennsylvania. After her first load, she and a young black boy were returning to Montgomery to get another load. A car of 4 men pulled alongside her car and one of the men in the back seat shot Mrs. Luizo in the head. The other man in the back seat was an FBI informant.

At the trial of the shooter, the defense lawyer asked the informant if he had been a member of the KKK. After admitting he was, the lawyer asked, "Didn't you take an oath never to testify against another klansman?" "Yes." "So, we know you were lying about that. How can we believe you when you point out this man as the killer?" On the basis of this defense argument the jury found the shooter "not guilty!"

Soon after it became known I had gone to support Dr. King's march, I was asked to come to League City and explain to 150 senior high youth why would anyone do a thing like that. I agreed and took a small book of an 11-year-old black girl's description of trying to go to a white school in Arkansas. A man named Faubus was governor of Arkansas at the time. I walked around among the senior high students reading the girl's words. She got off the city bus at the corner to face a jeering crowd of white people. They were cursing and spitting on her from both sides of the sidewalk. It got worse when she turned up the walkway to the school building. Governor Faubus was standing in the doorway with State Guard soldiers around him with bayonets fastened on their guns. The governor told her she could not enter the school in spite of the Federal Judge's ruling that she could.

As she turned to walk back down the walkway to the street, the crowd grew stronger with it cursing her. She wrote that she had the crazy idea that if she could just get to the bench on the corner where she got off the bus, she would be safe. The next day she was escorted back to enter the school with 8 Federal Marshalls accompanying her. Also, the President of The United States had National Guardsmen there to control the crowd.

After reading this 11-year-old girl's story, I stepped up into the pulpit in League City United Methodist Church and said, "History will record that the criminals on the bridge in Selma were Sheriff Jim Clark and his officers that were beating the black marchers down for days." At this one statement, a young man jumped to his feet from the audience to demand I take that statement back. He said he knew these officers. He had been with them to meals at his grandmother's home. He claimed they were good Christian men, and he wanted me to take back what I had said about them. I acknowledged to him that I did not know a single one of those officers, but I knew history would judge them as the criminals in the event.

After a few moments of disagreement and learning he was not a senior high but had brought some senior high students, I asked him if he would wait until our meeting with senior high students was over to talk with me. He agreed and sat down.

After the meeting, he was waiting and we talked for a long time about what was true and what was not true. I finally told him I had to drive several hours to get home and opened my car door to get in. He said, "Before you go, I owe you this story. I always wanted to be a clergyman, and to start me out as a student Pastor they assigned me to three small churches around Selma. On the second Sunday in February—Race Relations Sunday—Methodist Pastors were supposed to say something about race relations. He said he merely said, 'we do need to reexamine our relations to the 'colored' race.'" The six men in the congregation all stood up, raised their offering envelopes over their heads, tore them up, threw them on the floor, and walked out of the service.

That Sunday night, a committee of members from all three churches came to say to him that if he didn't leave town, they would kill me. He said to me, "I ran because I believed they really would have killed me. And I gave up my dream of being a clergyman." I thanked him for sharing that with me and agreed with him that there are people that would kill over this issue. I drove home wondering how any person who would challenge a guest speaker would have a story like that to tell and want to tell it after his own behavior in the sanctuary.

I had two problems as a clergyman in the Texas Annual Conference of The United Methodist church. Many of the leading clergymen in our Annual Conference were strongly against black people and they also hated the Ecumenical Institute and hated me for using it. None of them could tell me why. I asked, "Have you ever met Joseph Mathews, heard him speak, read something he wrote?" The answer was always "No!" Actually, the meanest people I have experienced in my life were those irrational clergymen. They would go out of their way to show this hatred and threaten to destroy my chances of getting a better appointment. One of them called the Lay Witness group leader the night before I moved to his church saying, "Don Sinclair is the very devil himself, and he is moving into your parsonage. You do everything you can to get him out as soon as you can. He will ruin your church!"

I would not have known this except two sensible young couples in that group came to see me together six months later to tell me about it. They had put their heads together and planned to watch me—one couple would go to everything I recommended, and the other couple would not. After six months of meeting and discussing everything, they made this appointment with me to say, "We think you are about the most perfect Pastor we have

41

ever seen. Why would anyone call to say that about you?" "I have some idea of who might do that, but I don't have time or the ability to stop it."

Then I asked them to do me a favor and never defend me in the presence of the leader of that group. They said they actually were preparing to do that and wondered why I would ask them not to do that. I replied, "Because the leader of your group is not a well man and will likely go off on you like a madman—even to cursing you and calling you names." They were shocked that I thought that would take place. I expressed the desire that they did not have to have that happen. But they spoke up to defend me to him and he cursed them and tore the group up. His wife went crying around asking everyone to come back to "group" and "let it be the way it used to be", but they would have nothing to do with him after that. Of course, I get his blame for it.

One of the young men in the four who originally came to tell me about this was in business with his father. They owned a company that took the undersea cable and covered it with waterproof covering for use on the ocean floor. They enlarged their shop and the company that helped arrange their shop gave every one of their employees psychological testing. That company asked the two business partners to have a conversation with them about one of their employees. He stopped by to tell me that the conversation was about the same guy who led that Lay Witness group. Their warning to the owners was that this man should always get written orders from the bosses because he will use some excuse to do things his own way otherwise. The young son wanted to know how I knew this about this guy so quickly. I shared with him that I had learned that sometimes the crazier you are the easier it is to be mistaken for a person of great faith and you can be allowed to volunteer yourself as a leader in the Church. That particular man became a Lay Pastor and received several small appointments as Pastor before he died. I called no one to tell them their Pastor was an emotionally disturbed man. I did feel relief when he died not many years later. My problem was that I knew there were others as bad or worse than he was.

Shortly after I became a member of the Bishop's staff in Adult Training, one of these came to me with one of his sermons printed out. He said he wanted to become a great preacher and he thought I would be the one to critique his sermons and make him a great preacher. The sermon was full of charges that most of the professors in Perkins School of Theology were Communists. His theology was full of claims that there were little demons floating around people's heads trying to get into their brains. I cautioned him and asked him about this belief. He even asked me, "Haven't you ever listened to people and wondered where all their strange ideas came from?"

He really had me there because I was sitting there looking at him wondering where all his strange ideas came from! I told him he would have to recruit someone else to work with him. Interesting though, he didn't live very long after that either.

For most of my life I stepped up to speak out in favor of things most of the Pastors or lay members of The Annual Conference were not in favor of it. That means I was a part of the minority and lost many battles. I spoke in favor of women Pastors, equal standing of Black Pastors and members, and the ongoing battle over declaring homosexual persons incompatible with the Christian Faith. This battle burst into a debate in the General Conference of The Methodist Church when the Bishops wanted to get a resolution in The Book of Discipline—our basic law book. The Bishops only preside over the General Conference. They do not get to vote or debate on issues. This was their effort to get a gentle word of recognition that we are aware we have homosexual members and that they are important to the Church, too.

But the seething hatred and fears of the heterosexual members burst out in a hateful debate which changed the Bishop's friendly statement into, "The homosexual lifestyle is incompatible with The Christian Faith." And it proceeded to limit the leadership roles homosexuals could be elected to. The year was 1972, at almost the exact time the National Boards of Psychiatrists and Psychologists voted to remove homosexuality from their diagnostic book declaring it was not a condition to be diagnosed or treated as a disease. It was to be seen as a natural birth condition like heterosexuality that some persons are born with, and, as such, it could not be changed. In their anger, they forgot that the New Testament declares ALL our lives to be incompatible with the Christian Faith. We Methodists preach that we are all moving toward perfection, but no one dares to claim they have reached perfection. So, it is very strange when one majority group of United Methodists begin to declare themselves better than another group. But, at this moment, this wonderful Church—which I think is the greatest Church ever created—is debating how to "split up" over homosexuality. The real issue, though, is how to "split up" AND TAKE OUR BEAUTIFUL BUILDINGS WITH US!

The traditional/standing rule is that the titles to land and buildings legally remain with The Annual Conference Trustees. Today—this very week, August 18, 2020—some of the Pastors and congregations who do not like homosexuals, want to separate themselves from United Methodists who care about homosexuals. Which would not be difficult at all, EXCEPT THAT THOSE CONGREGATIONS WHO HAVE BOUGHT LAND AND BUILT BIG BEAUTIFUL BUILDINGS ON IT WANT TO TAKE THE PROPERTY WITH THEM.

This would be the perfect time to include my last appointment and the ministry that the congregation created for its community. I became the Pastor of Bering Memorial United Methodist Church in Houston in June 1986. Earlier, during the 1960s, this church of German Immigrants had a very large congregation. Houston City Councilmen and several wealthy families were in its membership. They asked their pastor if they could hold a meeting on Sunday afternoon with him to discuss a particular disturbance they had been witnessing. It seemed local people in this Montrose area of Houston were disturbed by hippies and homosexuals that were settling around them. Bering members wanted to ask "why is this disturbing to these congregations?"

After looking at the related bible verses and getting clear what the issues were, Bering Memorial United Methodist Church decided in the 1960s that they saw no justification for such objections and would never discriminate against any of these people. Word got around and a few gay people checked it out. Most of those remained members and, by the time I arrived in 1986 there were many people of a variety of sexual orientations in leadership roles. There were about 40 white-headed German Immigrants still there in the membership. I buried most of those during my 10 years there. I told my wife that when I looked out over those white-headed Immigrants, I knew I was looking at "The salt of the earth." I was so proud to know them. Then word got out that the new Pastor "loved old people!" I was glad they thought so because I did love them.

In August 1986, I asked about 20 of the leaders to meet with me to help look at the struggles the Church was having. We sat around a long table in the fellowship hall below the sanctuary. They were telling me they had 5 2-story buildings left from the glory days of a larger congregation. The 'flight to the suburbs' took their wealthiest people into west Houston to help develop new churches. Houston's economic crash came later than the rest of Texas' crash which killed jobs in Houston. Bering Church was $50,000.00 in debt and couldn't even pay the interest on the debt. At that moment the air conditioning went out where we were meeting and, in the sanctuary, above. The man sitting next to me, Bayless, groaned, "There goes another air handler and we can't have it fixed!" I asked him to translate that a little more so I would know what had happened and why we can't fix it.

He said there are 11 huge fans blowing air over water pipes in all these buildings. It costs $18,000 to have one of them repaired. We have just repaired 2 of them for $36,000, which ran our indebtedness up to $50,000+ which we are unable to pay.

In our planning, they had told me about a "Grand Plan" that some of the members in the group had been working on for 2 years to answer the question: "Should we remain here in this location or sell it and move somewhere else and start over?" They handed me a copy of this printed/published study that had been led by a wonderful lady, Esther Houser.

We had been there an hour, so I began to respond to their situation with all the wisdom I could muster from my many years experience. I began with: "I have two questions for you." Number one is, "Does the Lord of History need a church on this street corner?" They burst into a "YES!" without hesitation, which startled me. Next is the question "Why does the Lord of History needs a church on this street corner?" Again, they burst out in one voice "AIDS!" I told them I had never seen a congregation as clear as they are about why they are here. I began to "context" them with the clear truth about our situation, which I declared was a 'good' situation to be in. I told them I did not know much about AIDS, but they did, and we were going to put together a huge plan doing what the AIDS victims needed and how people should respond to AIDS.

One of them asked about the air conditioning problem. I called it a gift to us because people use to go to church here, even in August, without air conditioning. We need a sign that WE are serious about this ministry, and attending church without air conditioning was the sign of our seriousness. I asked Bayless on my right if the beautiful stained-glass windows in the sanctuary were pointed at the top. He said they were. I asked him to locate the screws that prevented them from swinging open like they used to. We were going back to using paper fans with messages on them. All the former members had that we wouldn't have, were the small electric fans on the walls, etc. We could even rustle up some large fans to place around in the sanctuary. I mentioned how wonderful we had 5 2-story buildings not being used because we do not have to go raise money to build buildings. Then—the planning.

I told them we were going to begin planning our ministry and program. I told them that any idea was acceptable WITHOUT CRITICISM. No one was to speak against any idea or to ask how we were going to pay for it. Just let the ideas float to the top of your mind and blurt them out. We put together the finest plan I have ever seen. We could start a Spiritual Support Group free to all patients, parents, and all helpers. To handle the fear of AIDS we would have the patients bring covered dishes to this Spiritual Support Group. For professional care of patients, parents, and caregivers, we would start a free Counseling Center. We established a free Day Care for adult patients with a nurse on duty to make sure patients took their pills on time all day. Then, the wildest thing of all. We opened up the ground floor of what used to be a children's building for Sunday School and created a free Dental Clinic for AIDS patients.

When this one came up, I asked my dentist who recommended it why this was so important. He gave me quite an education about homosexuals often neglect their teeth and the easiest place to spot the AIDS virus was in the soft gums of the mouth. He added that even gay dentists couldn't risk it being known they worked on AIDS patients in their chairs. All their regular patients would leave them.

So, we sent out 85 invitations to Dentists who would help us set up a dental clinic in our church buildings. 84 Dentists came to the first meeting and stayed to help secure equipment. I was told to tell this first group that we needed an x-ray machine—that we had one, but it "floats." A young man stood up immediately to say, "Sir, my entire family makes its living repairing x-ray machines. Your x-ray machine will be the finest in the city, guaranteed!" This was our experience all the time.

During our planning and scrambling to get everything set up I was looking for some mysterious miracle that would provide emotional stimulation and conversation among all our workers and beyond. I found one when we went into the building where the dental clinic would be. It had been class rooms for the large Sunday School with an office. Inside this office, we found a large iron safe that was larger than the door of the closet it was in. A few remarks were made about how impossible it would be to get the huge safe moved out.

At midnight that night, I loaded my large car jack into my car, gently removed the framing around the door so there would be no scars in the wood. I pushed the safe backward enough to get my car jack under the front of it, pulled it down, rolled it out of the office into the hallway, and set it against the wall. The doorway framing was carefully replaced exactly as it had been. The next morning one of the people rushed into our office area expressing shock that the safe he had seen trapped in the closet the night before was setting out in the hall. No one had any idea how that was possible. It was years before I told anyone how it happened. We needed a sign that impossible things could be done.

There were many other things that began to happen. I called on the President of the plumber's union about noon. He was standing in his office with a guest he was taking to lunch. I told him about our need to arrange for some plumbing for our dental clinic. They both went back to the church with me to see the building. I discovered that the other man with him was head of the plumbing inspection for Houston. They were enthusiastic about our plan, and we had no problems in the process of making Sunday School rooms into a dental clinic. Within a week, a plumber showed up with all the "black pipe" we would need for the gas lines and half his salary paid by the plumber's union.

St. Luke's United Methodist Church, which has a whole wing of its buildings named after a man who was once a member of Bering Memorial, gave us $5000.00. We went out to secure the copper tubing, etc. for the water and airlines in the Dental Clinic. We got it loaded on the truck and stopped at the gate to pay. The owner of the plumbing supplies business came running out to ask if this was for the Dental Clinic for AIDS patients being put in that church. When we said, "Yes," he asked for the papers, tore them up, and said, "These people get anything they need and they do not have to pay for it." We became the darling of the town of Houston. We had trouble spending our money anywhere.

Early in our efforts to find ways to make things happen, one of the choir members won Houston's radio station's contest where you went chasing over Houston following clues you had to figure out what the clues meant and find what object was hidden. The prize was very huge, and she wanted us to meet the armored car in front of the church to receive the "tithe" on the amount she had won. So, we had our treasurer out there with a deposit slip already filled out when the armored truck pulled up and guards with shotguns fanned out around it. The choir member handed our treasurer the "tithe" and both took off swiftly—our treasurer to the bank, the winning girl to select her favorite color of the convertible. She had to spend all the money that Saturday, but she could put about $25,000 into a CD.

Her winnings enabled a long-awaited overhauling of our sanctuary. The choir got to give direction to the work needed in the choir area, and two very talented gay partners took on the work on the sanctuary. You will not believe this, but I will say it anyway. Saturday was declared WORKDAY for many months for volunteers directed by the two gay partners. They used 30-foot ladders to reach the ceiling—a dozen ladders at a time for volunteers to use. Most of their time was spent going up and down those high ladders with their paint supply. They had to move the ladders over a few feet at a time. AT NO TIME WAS PAINT SPILLED OR DROPPED ON THE PEWS DURING THE 6 MONTHS OF THE CEILING WORK!

This was followed by additional work to re-cover all our pews. Funds were raised by everyone present each Sunday putting a paperclip on a $1.00 bill. One of the two guys who supervised the sanctuary project would cover as many pews each week as the offering would allow. Everyone began to come into the sanctuary to count how many pews were completed and how many were yet to be covered—how many more $1.00 they would have to drop into the collection plate. The counting game was a lot of fun and was finished in record time. The talented man covering the pews located the expensive material used on the kneeling cushions on the altar. Out came the paperclips and $1.00 again to include that to match the pews.

When the 2 workers assigned the sanctuary came to the floor of the Foyer, they wanted to refinish the floor and paint seashells in the four corners. The problem was we were holding Holy Week services, which were very special at Bering Church. They figured out how much time each coating of varnish and paint would take to dry, and, on Maundy Thursday when we had three services, they came early. First to recondition the floor and varnish it, and rope it off until the next Maundy Service was scheduled, and take down the ropes and ribbons they used to keep people off it. As soon as the service was over, they would rope it off again to give it another coating to dry. This went on all day Thursday, and, by Friday they had painted the shells in the four corners of the Foyer, and, it was beautiful.

I had the joy of standing in front of this congregation praising them and thanking them for being the great people they were and had always been. When I had a chance, I enjoyed standing in front of their parents to say what great children they had raised and how much their children loved them as their parents. Doctors and lawyers would invite me over to their homes to MEET their parents, because what I thought of their son or daughter would change what they thought of their son or daughter.

Besides the members doing so much so well we got help from all corners. There was a man named Frank who owned a bar in the Rice University area. He came up to see what he could do. He was never a member of Bering, but he discovered we had the usual problem of keeping large spoons for the kitchen. He got a huge briefcase, bought about 30 big spoons, brought them to the Spiritual Support Group every Wednesday night, and stuck them into the 'covered dishes' brought by the members. After the meal, he would collect the 30 big spoons, wash them, and place them in the huge briefcase and take them home. Frank did this for the 10 years I was there. I'm not sure how long he did that. He would also let Bering Church use his bar for anything they wanted.

Some of the greatest conversions came at their son's funeral. We buried people who were not members of Bering but had been great leaders there. At their funerals, I would have 3 or 4 young adults come to the front and tell everyone how much this person had meant to them and why. Without fail, parents would come down to the altar to thank me for letting them know what their child was doing as a churchman.

Two special stories of this and I must move on with this paper. Early on my arrival at Bering, our Lay Leader came to my office to talk. I asked him what his father said to him about his being gay. "Son, you're going to Hell!' which is what any decent Deacon in the Baptist church is supposed to say." This young 28-year-old was a sick man—an engineer working at odd jobs to keep afloat financially. When he would get sick enough to have to be in the hospital, his father would come down from Lubbock to stay in his apartment to see about him. At his funeral, with 4 young men giving witness to his son's greatness, this Baptist Deacon brought his wife with him to the altar and, while weeping, thanked me for giving their son back to them. Because he was doing the same thing back home when he was young, and they had wasted 10 years being ashamed of him. I always encouraged such parents to not let other parents waste the lives of their gay children.

Second, a father drove over from Louisiana with Baptist women—friends of his new Baptist wife. We were planning for his gay son's funeral, but he was not participating. The three Baptist women had a lot to say, but they were not being helpful. I finally just told the father what we usually do at Bering Church. He agreed, it seemed, just to get this session over. After the service, he rushed up to me at the altar without the 3 women and asked if he could talk to me privately. I said, "Sure. Let's go back into my office." As we walked into my office, he was saying he was so confused about things. He said his wife says her stepson was burning in Hell, her Pastor says he is burning in Hell, but I don't know whether there is a Hell or not. . . .." I turned and grabbed him on the shoulder and said, "Hang on to that thought!" It startled him so he said, "Which thought?" He was not sure which thought he was on running down his list of confusions. I said, "I'm going to tell you something I would be shot for saying in some places, but I want you to hear it said by a Pastor with over 40 years in the pulpit. There has never been a place the Church calls Hell! No one is burning in Hell because there is no such place and there never has been!" He stood looking at me for a moment and said, "Well, I'll be damned! I've wondered about that all my life!" We sat for a moment while he 'collected' himself to repeat, "Well, I'll be damned! I've been a Methodist all my life and my first wife was a Methodist. We didn't hear much about Hell there. But I married this Baptist lady recently, and they are really strong on Hell. So, what I will do is go on back home with my new Baptist wife and attend church with her, but when that preacher cuts loose on Hell, I will just grin to myself and know he is wrong."

Then he got around to the question, "Why does the church use Hell so much? Where did they get the idea and why do they keep on using it?" I shared with him that it fits into the understanding of the world before the Christian Church was born. "In the creation story in the bible, they believed the blue sky above us was water that God just pulled up there and holds it. In the story of Noah's ark, God lets go of that water above us and drowned almost everything. Also, there are places where we can still observe hot lava gushing out of the earth. Religions try to give understandings of all this mystery so that it works well for the religion. When religion gets something wrong, we have great difficulty 'unpreaching' what our ancestors taught us was God's holy truth. Once we drag God into it, we are stuck with it for thousands of years or more. But Hell has been very useful for the Church to frighten people and make them do what the Church thinks they should do. Don't you think it has worked pretty well for the Church during your lifetime?"

His final response was, "When I came over here to my son's funeral, I thought it was going to be the worst day of my life. But your service at this church and talking with you, it has become the very best day of my life. Thank you for removing all that burden I came here with. I feel so much better about everything. I just wish I could have seen my son as your church sees him. Thank you, sir, for a wonderful day." I asked him to look around and help another family see the greatness in their gay children. Help them not waste the years you did with your son. He left with a joyful heart and his new Baptist wife and her 2 Baptist women friends.

Federal Judge Woodrow Seals had always had an interest in me and my ministries. He got Dr. John Henry Faulk, the professor and successful play write, interested in me and Bering Church. He came out to meet with the

Spiritual Support Group to do some research for a play he wanted to write for the stage in Houston. He said he wanted to involve his Jewish friend, Carolyn Farbe, in this. He did this but then John Henry became very ill. He was able to come later to our worship service when Bering Memorial United Methodist Church declared his Jewish friend, Carolyn Farbe, a "Bering Angel." We did this for anyone we heard was making a creative response to AIDS.

It was his friend Carolyn Farbe who really put us on the map in Houston. Many of the people working on Bering's Aids Ministries did not know each other at all. The Cadillac Bar wanted to help in some way, so they threw a party with free drinks and food. I began announcing where Cadillac Bar was located until the gay members told me everyone but me already knew where that Bar was.

Carolyn Farbe got the large stage, Alley Theater, downtown Houston to give us over $100,000 from their October 1987 opening night proceeds. We had the Dental Clinic ready and ordered supplies the next week. Those members at Bering got permission to use the park across from the theater and got 14 chefs to bring their equipment out there and prepare their favorite deserts for the people as they came out of the theater. Then, one of the workers on this project learned there was a "Last Lucile Ball" a few blocks away. He went down and got the 8 models modeling their red "Beehive" hairdos to come down and do their show for the people as they were having their deserts. Then all the Bering people had to take down the lights, clean up the park before going to bed—hours of work. The next morning, they were in Church, and I asked if someone would help me figure out if Houston gave us a party last night or did we give Houston a party? I loved those people! They were great at being The Church!

That dental clinic was opened October 1987. It is still there as 2021 approaches. It treats 1000 people every month—AIDS patients. It was run for 2 years on voluntary dentists who were just glad to have a place to send AIDS patients. The first Dentist we hired to run it is still there now—September 2020. He has become a global lecturer on how to deliver low-cost dental services to AIDS patients.

One day, just after he returned from Beijing, China for the second time, the wife of the Chinese Consulate in Houston walked into my office to get help finding a place where she could study English. I made some calls and located a place she could go. As we stood up, I asked if she were walking. She said she was and I offered to drive her there, but she refused. I then asked if she had time to meet one of my staff that had just returned from Beijing.

I took her over to meet our Dentist. She asked him what he was doing in China. He said he was teaching Dentist how to care of people with AIDS. She was puzzled and said, "But we do not have AIDS in China!" I thought we were about to cause an international incident, but the Dentist smiled and said, "Sometimes OUR OWN governments do not tell us the whole truth about what's really going on." I thought that was profound and that our Dentist should be an ambassador.

My mind swirls as I try to think of all that I should attempt to write in this paper. There was so very much that happened daily and weekly that it would be impossible for me to share even a small portion. But I want you to know about Rosie. Kathy and I never had a daughter, but Rosie was the closest thing to a daughter. I met her one afternoon at her sister's apartment. Her sister was helping me with my income tax report when Rosie rushed in after school to pick up something. Gloria said, "This is Rosie, my younger sister. Rosie this is Don." Rosie greeted me and left in a hurry. I didn't know Gloria's family and asked where Rosie lived. Gloria had difficulty answering that. She told me her mother had been in the mental hospital in Austin for 10 years and she had to get Rosie out of the dangerous situation with her father and three brothers at home. Since Gloria's apartment was small and she had two half-grown sons there just wasn't room for Rosie to live with them. She was living temporarily with some friends.

A few months later, after being in the mental hospital for 10 years, their mother was 'dropped off' by a bus from Austin because the mental hospital there was running out of money. While filling up with gasoline in the Montrose area where Bering Church is located, I saw Rosie walking down the street a block over and going into a Jr. High School close by. She came out toward me down a street one block over. I circled down that street and stopped to talk. She was taking her younger brother with her to look at an apartment she was thinking of renting. I went with them the three blocks down (three blocks from my parsonage), but the apartment was too small for the three of them. I took them home. She and her mother were living in the 2nd-floor apartment of a building that had its first floor burned out. There was not a chair in their living space. Her mother sold roses one at a time on the streets and/or Sunday newspapers in front of large grocery stores.

Rosie was 15, working two jobs to get her mother a better place to live. I talked with her about how I could help her. One thing we thought of was to help her with washing and drying their clothes. So, each week I would pick Rosie up with the pile of clothes, take her to our Parsonage and lock her safely in to use our washer and dryer while she did her school work. I learned Rosie was one of the four ROTC Commanders in Houston and was used at her school to train the ROTC students for marching contests in Houston and nationally.

When Kathy got home from her teaching job, I told her about all that Rosie was up against, and I could not stand to see a young girl up against so many problems and making all the right decisions. So, Rosie moved into our Parsonage with a room of her own with a desk and a chair to do her studies on. We got Kathy a new car and kept her car for Rosie to use. So, for two years, we had a 'live-in' daughter. I'll spare you hundreds of things you will have to sit and get me to tell sometime. But Rosie married a dentist who was a major finishing his time in the Army. They now live in the Austin, Texas area, and I think both are very successful and doing well.

I will tell you about the young man who came into my office, plopped down in a chair and said, "I am told you can tell me what I am doing here!" I had never seen him before, so I asked him to tell me what is going on in his life. He told me that he was a devout Muslim who faithfully attended all services at his Temple in Houston. He said he was a waiter and had saved $4,000 and wondered if that would see him through hospital costs until he died. He had to die alone in Houston because if his mother back home found out, she would come get him. "I am gay and I have AIDS, and if you think Christians are sometimes mean you should see what happens when Muslims hear that information. My entire family back home would be ostracized by all the other Muslims for the rest of their lives. No one would even speak to them forever. I can't let that happen to my mother, so I have to die quietly here in Houston without anyone ever knowing." I have written this story down for future publishing pieces, and I named it, "The Bravest Man I Have Ever Met."

That happened on a Wednesday morning, so I told him I now know why he is here. "You return here tonight at 7:00 o'clock and I will introduce you to the next 75 members of your new family. This is a kind and loving United Methodist Christian Church and no one will bother you about your beliefs. You do not bring a dish of food this first time. You are our guest for dinner. Your $4,000 will not see you through, but this group will see you through all the way."

Ralph had a little trouble believing what I was telling him, but I reassured him about his being in the right place. He showed up, and of course I made sure he met some people that would involve him with others. What surprised me was that he met and became a close friend with the only Jewish member of our group. Ralph was 24 and the Jewish man was 64 years old. Every Wednesday night they ate together and went to "groups" together.

We called the group a "Spiritual Support Group", and when I would go to other churches I would sometimes be asked about the word "Spiritual." I would tell them this story about Ralph and Joseph—the Muslim and the Jew joining and finding fellowship with the group and with each other. Thoughtful people sometimes worry about what people mean using the word "Spiritual," because it is often used in relation to religious beliefs that are unacceptable. But this story represents real human fellowship that is glorious to behold.

There is another part of Ralph's and Joseph's participation that I really love. At the beginning of each Wednesday night we always announce that there will be a Christian Communion service immediately following group meetings that was for anyone who wanted to remain and attend. It was to be held in the big parlor because it was away from the other rooms. People leaving would have to retrace their steps back to the parlor. We did this to make sure the only people present were people who wanted to go to the extra service back in the parlor. The Communion service lasted 10 to 15 minutes and was conducted by me or the clergyman who ran our Counseling Center, Rev. Troy Plummer. Some of our participants were not sure they would live through another week which makes Holy Communion a more important event in their lives.

The strange thing was that Ralph, the Muslim man, and Joseph, the Jewish man would always come to this intensely Christian service. They never missed! When serving the elements of Jesus' crucifixion and death, we would always say, "If for any reason you do not wish to receive these elements just wave us on by when we come to you." Ralph and Joseph would always wave us on by. I knew that one day I would have a chance to ask them why they came. When that time came, they said, "You and/or Troy always make a brief sentence statement about why you are serving those elements—what they mean in life. We come to hear those brief words. They are never the same. You always change the expressions, and we enjoy those brief words."

Joseph had family around him, but Ralph had only our group. My wife, Kathy and I knew when he had to go to the hospital and came there to see him. It was during one of his hospital visits that he said to us, "My mother is coming to visit me. I have to bluff my way out of this hospital and see if I can manage to stay on my feet for 2 weeks to keep her from knowing I'm sick." I pulled out one of my cards to hand him saying if you need us, call and we will help you with anything we can. To which Ralph replied, "You do not understand, Don. That card has a cross and the name of your Christian church on it. I must never have anything like that in any of my clothes. I may be saying, 'I can never see you again!'" Kathy and I both hugged him and wished him well and told him that we loved him. We all three parted crying. I do not know what happened to Ralph, but I did know he was the bravest man I had ever known and that he loved his mother very much. That was about 1993. I never heard from him again, but I also know he experienced real love and acceptance that was bigger than the hatred our religions often teach against other religions.

Kathy retired from teaching in 1991 because she wanted to work with this Spiritual Support Group. One night, while we sat eating, a middle-aged woman came from the rather dark entrance into our Fellowship Hall with a small thin young man. Kathy saw her, pushed her chair back and walked to this woman and embraced her, and welcomed her and her son. The Support Group was eating, so Kathy made a place for this woman and her son to sit with her to eat. Her son had just been dismissed from the hospital, and the nurses had told the mother to take her son to our Spiritual Support Group. She came a stranger to us. Her other children had withdrawn from her son, Kelly, and she had lost her husband a few years earlier. She chose to be a loving mother to her son but she was all alone.

Because of that hug by Kathy, she and Mary Parker became sisters for life without a word spoken—just a hug. Mary and Kelly had found an accepting and loving family of 100 people on that fateful night. Mary and Kelly joined Bering Church and Kathy asked her to help her with a "garage sale" type of project to raise money for Bering's AIDS ministries. It turned out that Mary Parker had some connections with homes where parents had died and the children wished to sell their house. Suddenly this "garage sale" found fine furniture available from these fine homes because Mary had worked out an arrangement to prepare the homes for sale if Bering Church could have the furnishings. So, the funds from this increased, and many people were needed to move the furniture and clean the houses. A bit of humor developed. When people joined Bering Church and the ritual of welcoming new members was finished a new question was added, "Do you own a pickup truck?" If they said, "Yes," they were assigned to Mary Parker to help haul furniture.

Kathy and I retired in 1996, but Mary Parker has become one of the very special members of Bering Church. Her work raises $80,000 per year for Bering Church. She is one of the most beloved people among many in the Bering congregation. She says she is surprised that her greatest vocation would be selling other people's junk.

But, I'm not through telling you about this amazing congregation. Kathy and I moved to Coldspring, 75 miles north of Houston. We had purchased land and wanted to build a concrete geodesic dome retirement home. We enjoyed going back to visit Bering each month and attending Pflag Houston (Parents & Friends of Lesbians and Gays) which met Sunday afternoon. One month, I went on crutches because I had damaged a sciatic nerve repairing the roof of my son's trailor. The Bering members had never seen me disabled in any way. So, even though I had retired several years earlier, they decided to help me finish that retirement home. I had the concrete roofing up and the inside walls for the 2nd story finished. It was ready to have sheetrock on the outside walls and a stair railing built.

So, a team of Bering members prepared musical programs and put them on around town to raise about $30,000 and came up to finish our home. We moved into it in 2005 and held the party I promised them. I asked a gay man who was forced out of the ministry, to come and lead the blessing service on our new home.

About 15 years after I retired from my 46 years of service in The United Methodist Church, I was walking alone out of Luby's restaurant in the Montrose area. I heard someone behind me call my name. I stopped to face a very healthy-looking young man who wanted to thank me for what we did at Bering Methodist Church. He said, "You would not remember me. I was not a member of your church, but I came there to Wednesday night Spiritual Support Group. I thought my life was over and I was planning on suicide. But what you guys were doing there really saved my life. I was so surprised to see you in that restaurant after all these years and I just wanted to thank you for what you and your Church have done for me and so many other people."

ADDENDUM

A few things that need to be shared about my life as the youngest child of Joseph and Lula Kate to show the struggle I had with some of the leadership of The Texas Annual Conference of our United Methodist Church and some of the things I achieved in spite of this.

Many of our leaders hated Joseph Mathews who started The Ecumenical Institute in Chicago, Illinois without ever reading his writings or hearing him speak. So, I couldn't tell them that some of the things I did that drew praise from the Pastors and laymen alike was what I had learned from The Ecumenical Institute.

For instance, a staff meeting of people who had conference offices was asked by our bishop to plan district meetings where the staff would help the Pastors focus on "Mission" as the new image of the Church. The first suggestion was one of us would need to prepare to explain where the Church had been and how we got to this moment. No one felt they could do that and we were about to proceed without this part when I said, "I will do that." After a few moments for the shock to wear off, the chairman asked me "Don, how long will it take you to do that?" My immediate answer was, "Seven minutes." Everyone was shocked at my definiteness, but I was assigned that task.

What they didn't know (and I couldn't tell them) was in the fourth lecture of the Religious Studies 1 (RS-1) of The Ecumenical Institute's Academy there is a seven-minute part that does exactly that—reviews 2000 years of church history and projects the image for the Church of the future as "Mission". We had practiced that at 5:00 o'clock every Tuesday morning in this very room (which they always complained about) in preparation for teaching RS-1 (which they hated me for doing). But, at the first meeting with the Pastors, I was introduced to start us out.

The Pastors crowed around me after the meeting with remarks like, "Sinclair, we always hate coming to these meetings because we don't think anything significant will happen, but your diagram of the first 2000 years of the Church made this meeting worthwhile!" At our next staff meeting, the chair asked, "Don, where did you learned how to do that?" I told him I had stolen it from some source I had run across. His response was, "Well, I think we should get another of the staff to do that part at our next meeting. Hooper Haygood, why don't you take that part for our next District meeting?" Hooper agreed, but 3 days before our next District meeting with Pastors, Hooper came to my office (which was the smallest one in the building) to say, "Don, I don't believe I can do that opening part you did last time. Why don't when I'm introduced to do that, I just simply introduce you to do that?" The results were always the same at the District meetings.

This infuriated our staff chairman. So, he assigned Wallace Shook to take that part at our 3rd District meeting. Again, 3 days before the meeting, Wallace came down to my office to say he liked what I did and, "let's handle it like you and Hooper did. When they introduce me to do it, I will simply introduce you to do it." So, that's the way it went for all our District meetings.

I was always proud to be related to The Ecumenical Institute. Their primary goal was to find the worst ghetto in Chicago and figure out how to recreate "humanness" in that community. They latched on to some deserted seminary buildings across Eisenhower freeway from Sears tower on the north side of Chicago. My whole family attended many of their July Research Assemblies with 500 people from all over the world present. It took EI eight years to accomplish their "Mission" in "5th City."

Each of our four sons attended their 2-month Academy after graduating from High School. Our first son, David, joined their staff after graduating college. He was assigned their "Children's Structures" for two years after which he was assigned to the Religious House in Anchorage, Alaska. He talked his Houston girlfriend into driving up there and marrying him. They raised two grandchildren there, and their son, the new Joe Sinclair, and his wife, Anya, have our first great-grandchild, Greta. Kathy and I recently made the trip to Alaska to marry their daughter, Kate.

Our second son, Robert, attended seminary and recently retired as Pastor in the same area of Texas I served. He married Mary Gingrich, a gifted musician from Missouri. She played the organ and piano for the church and local school students entering statewide singing competitions. They have two of our grandchildren, Ben and Ann.

Our third son, Douglas, graduated High School in Canada and college in Houston with a degree in Computer Components. When he attended the EI Academy, he was asked to pick up several others who needed rides from Dallas and Memphis. I sat down with him to make sure he was clear that his primary goal was to get to the Academy in Chicago and the station wagon he would be driving was not a new vehicle. If he broke down anywhere, he was to solve the problem and call me to let me know where he had to leave the station wagon. Sure enough, the right rear wheel had caught on fire inside the hub. He found the largest car that would hold all their suitcases and made the one call to tell me he had left the station wagon at an Exon service station in Roan Oak, Arkansas.

I was Pastor of a small church in Corrigan, Texas. After taking a sabbatical to experience living in a Family Order to finish mine and Kathy's 20-year study of how to raise children. The Methodist Church makes you start over in small churches following a sabbatical. I asked a member of the church to drive me to Arkansas to repair and bring the station wagon home. I told him it would take all day. I had found the right wheel and axel on a car in the wrecking yard that I could quickly replace the entire right rear wheel in my station wagon. He wanted to see that done, so we took off early the next day. It took me about 20 minutes to take four bolts off and replace the rear axle and wheel assembly and begin our trip home.

Twice I was asked by members of the Corrigan church, "What are you doing in this little church?" First was the Superintendent of Schools. He asked me to come down to his office, and he asked me that question. I told him that The Methodist Church was the only organization I knew of that punished you for taking time off to improve yourself by making you "start over" with a small church assignment. He said, "I can believe that. I just knew you were an experienced and knowledgeable Pastor and couldn't understand why you had been appointed to this small congregation."

The second time it was a retiring couple from Houston who had moved to Corrigan. They called and asked me to come to their home. They said, "We moved up here and expected to find a young Pastor just starting his career, and we find you. Why were you assigned to Corrigan?" I told them the same thing.

Our fourth son, Stanley, was extremely gifted in music. When he was 14 years old the organist at East Bernard asked him to play the organ for two weeks so she could go on vacation. At the same moment, the organist was coaching Stanley her sister-in-law, who owned the Chevrolet, business asked me to come by her office. It was during the early 1970's when The Methodist Church was arguing at General Conference about homosexuality and what they would be allowed to do in the church. Her question was, "Tell me why I should not pick up that phone and call our bishop about this.

They are thinking of allowing homosexuals to teach in the Sunday School, and I don't think that should be allowed." Neither she nor I knew that my 14 year-old son being coached by her sister-in-law at that very moment was actually gay. We didn't learn that until he was murdered in Houston. The investigators ask if we knew our son was gay. That was between Christmas and New Year's, 1979.

Just so you know, several years ago I was in Chicago across town from the Ecumenical Institutes "5th City." I went by cab to visit the area again. A few of the residents remembered me coming to work with the staff there. About 20 of them wanted me to see the shopping center they had built. As we walked around to it one of the group said, "I think that policeman wants to talk to you." I looked around, and a policeman was standing outside his patrol car waving me over. His question was, "Are these people bothering you?" I reassured him they were all friends and that I had come to help with this community work many times. They want to show me their shopping center.

The officer said, "You might be able to help me understand the change here. I use to spend half my time chasing criminals down here. We would get several calls a week, but suddenly it stopped. We never get calls from this area now. Do you know why?" I was glad to explain how the Ecumenical Institute came here to do its research on how to restore humanness in a ghetto. They were taught they could not make a life blaming others for their situation. They needed to take responsibility for their entire community and find a way to solve all their own problems. I told him the story of taking a group of these "thugs" across town to check out prices of televisions, refrigerators, washing machines, etc. The prices in these wealthier areas cost less than in their community. They immediately got angry with their local merchants, but the Ecumenical Institute staff explained to them that the merchants in their community had higher insurance costs, had to put up gates and chains, etc. to protect their goods because they had a lot of things stolen. Their merchants had to charge more for everything in their community. Their problem was crime in their own community.

It took the Ecumenical Institute staff 8 years to complete their work in 5th City. Their real breakthrough came when Dr. Martin Luther King, Jr was killed. Their staff knew the burning would include some of their buildings and made plans for their response. All people who lived there were not to resist or fight with those who came to burn their apartments or workrooms. They were to step aside and bow to the burners as they came, set their fire, and as they left after setting the fire. All staff members would figure out how to put the fires out and let that be the end of it.

The next week the "thugs" came knocking on EI's door saying, "You have been telling us we do not really have control in this community and there would come a time when we realized it. We tried to stop these people from burning their own community down. We could not stop them, so, we are here to ask you about all that stuff you have been saying to us and what we can do about it." They were welcomed in and they listened to learn about people, community life, and that they had to work on all age's problems at the same time—not just children, then youth, then adults, then the elderly. The "thugs" went to work with new understandings about community life. The result is a community without the crime and everyone's problems are getting the caring attention needed. They work together for everyone's good.

Still, after many years, my problem is why did our leaders in our Texas Annual Conference of The United Methodist hate The Ecumenical Institute? I have been retired for 24 years and, I am glad to say, that leadership is dead and gone. The leadership now seems more natural and sensible. This paper could be much longer, but I have to stop somewhere. The children of Joseph Jarrell Sinclair and Lula Kate Evans, Welch, Sinclair have made their mark on this world, and this is their story.